D1347347

HAPPY LANDINGS

HAPPY LANDINGS

James Barclay

LINDSAY PUBLICATIONS

First published in 1998 by
Lindsay Publications
Glasgow

© James Barclay 1998

ISBN 1 898169 14 4

British Library Cataloguing-in-Publication Data
A Catalogue record for this book is available
from the British Library

Designed and typeset by Mitchell Graphics, Glasgow
Cover illustration by John Gahagan

Printed and bound in Finland by WSOY

ONE

THE WAR GREW IN INTENSITY AND THE GERMANS OCCUPIED MOST OF Europe. The Luftwaffe continued it's devastating raids over Britain. Glasgow was first hit by a night raid on September 18th 1940 and it continued until March 23rd 1943 when the last Heinkel flew home. Just two years previously, on the nights of 13th to 15th of March, 1941, Clydebank was pulverised by the German massed raid. Greenock was to get it two months later. But these raids only left the Scots with gritted determination to avenge. They still sang "We're gonny hang out our washing on the Seigfried Line" in the air-raid shelters, drowning out the groaning sounds of the engines above them...engines of destruction and death. The Glasweigans rolled up their sleeves and caught 'caurs' to work despite their interrupted sleep. They laughed and they cried and they loved. They loved behind blacked out windows, They shuffled home in the black-out, dodging Baffle Walls that stood on the pavement in front of tenement closes placed there to deflect blast. In the blacked-out city streets they dodged crawling cars that were stealthily wending their way along with only slits on their headlamps to illuminate their course. If the German bombers had done nothing, else they had invoked the wrath of Wullie McSorley, who lived with his sister, Annie, in their tenement home at 27, Well Street, in the Calton district of the city...just a stone's throw from 'Ra Barras' — the famous Glasgow market territory which ran down Kent Street from London Road to the Gallowgate swallowing up surrounding streets, including Gibson Street where the 'Steamie', or to give it its proper title, the Public Wash House, was. Wullie had been lifted by the news that the Germans crack general Erwin Rommel had been defeated at El Alamein, on November the fourth, 1942. If Rommel could be beaten, they could all be beaten, he reckoned. The news raised his spirits, coming just a little more than a year after Hitler had invaded Russia. The North British Locomotive works, which had switched to making tanks, now had a project, "Make a tank for Russia". The news heartened Wullie and he contributed the odd shilling when he could afford it. Annie's 'man', Big Sammy had been called up right away and served with the Pioneer Corps. He had been captured in France but, nae prison wull keep ma Sammy in for long!" Annie had defiantly said. And she proved correct. Sammy had made his escape but, after stealing a canoe at Calais, had taken a wrong turning crossing the Channel and was duly picked up by a Japanese gun boat in the Bay of Bengal. Living with bachelor Wullie and Annie was Annie's daughter, Rita who had recently married Rasputin Plunkett, now serving with His Majesty's Forces "Somewhere in England". Rita continued working as a 'clippie' on the Glasgow Corporation Trams at the Dalmarnock Depot, in Ruby Street. She HAD considered joining the Women's Land Army, attracted by the country life and the healthy diet that would come along with it. But had changed her mind as she would miss the camaraderie of the dusty tenement in Well Street where she was brought up. Annie was glad that Rita would stay on the 'caurs' and in the house. Next door, across the landing, Ina McLatchie was still grieving the death of her ninety year old father, Jake, a former thespian who once played opposite Rin-Tin-Tin, the great American dog actor, during a stint in Hollywood. Ina had made it clear that she fancied Wullie McSorley and once, sitting inside an air-raid shelter during an attack, had thought that her attentions were being reciprocated when Wullie, charmed by her home-made 'soday scones' had actually held her hand. But Wullie's slight deviation from his strong bachelor path came to nothing and a disappointed Ina was back on the hunting trail. The Luftwaffe had not come over for a few nights and Wullie decided to have an early night in bed. He retired to his room and, propping himself up against the pillows, switched on the bedside lamp and turned to page twenty-six and continued to read his tattered Dandy Annual which he had acquired at the 'Barras' the weekend previously. Satisfied that Desperate Dan had the situation well in hand, he smiled, switched off the lamp, snuggled under the blankets and was soon fast asleep. It was nine-forty six p.m. He awoke with a start at ten-twenty, the air-raid sirens wailing in the street. Annie was already dressed and put her head round the door.

"C'mon, Wullie," she snapped, "Fritz is here!"

Wullie leapt from his bed and, making sure his tasselled nightcap was in place and his long, flannel nightgown smoothed down, he hurried from the room, grabbed the two 'Wally dugs' from the mantleshelf and raced out and down the stairs after Annie. He shivered in the night chill as he hurried across the street and up the pend where the flat-topped, brick air-raid shelter stood. The damp shelter was already filling up and people, all wearing a variety of garments, from siren suits - one piece suits that slipped on and zipped all the way up the front - worn by folk in a hurry to housecoats over pyjamas. Wullie growled when he heard the strains of a mouth organ playing at the end of the shelter.

"There's always SOMEBODY wants ye tae sing," he moaned.

As the music continued he wished he had brought his Dandy Annual and sighed loudly when, after three hours, the 'All-Clear' siren screeched its welcome wail. As the shelter spilled out, Annie, her brows knitted, looked around her. She could see no sign of Ina McLatchie. Arriving back at the house, Wullie flopped on to a chair by the dining table. Annie made for the black-leaded range and put the kettle on the gas ring on top.

"Aw, thank God tae get hame! Ah thought the All-Clear would never come. Oh, this awful war! Where's it a' gonny end?"

She sadly shook her head.

"If they just let ME get in there," Wullie piped up, "Aye, me an' Big Sandy and Wee Erchie, we'd show them!"

His mind went back to World War One, when he served with pride with the Highland Light Infantry, the great H.L.I. Once more he saw himself marching down Sauchiehall Street, is McKenzie tartan kilt swinging in the breeze. Yes, if only he were a bit younger, he...and Sandy and Erchie would show them. With the thought clear in his mind, he couldn't contain himself. Leaping from his chair, he yelled, "Ower and at them boys, ower and at them!" He thrust his imaginary bayonet forward and was back once more in the muddy trenches of France.

"When the Jerries saw oor kilts flappin' n the wind," he went on, "they screamed in terror and turned an' ran for their lives."

"So did every lassie in Gallygate," Annie said with a wry smile.

Wullie ignored the facetious remark. "The Ladies from Hell, they called us," he said proudly.

"That's no' whit the lassies called youse," Annie said, still smiling.

"Aye, well," Wullie went on, "there's still life in the auld dug yet," he said, "Just put a bayonet in ma haun'... Ah'd show them!"

Annie let out a loud laugh.

"Wullie, you canny even cut a slice o' breid ye're that clumsy. The last time ye tried Ah telt ye tae be careful an' ye just turned an' gave me two fingers. It wisnae nice!"

"It's a gesture," Wullie said, sulkily, "loats o' people gie folk two fingers."

"No' in a jiffy bag they don't," Annie said coldly.

"Ach, well, they sewed them back on again up at the Royal. They are very clever doactors up there at the Royal Infirmary," Wullie retorted.

"Aye, right enough," Annie said, "Look whit they did for wee Tommy Maloney."

Wullie's eyebrows went up. "Whit aboot wee Tommy Maloney?"

"Well, "Annie said, "when he was a wean, he stuck his haun' in a dug's mooth and it chewed his thumb aff an' swallyed it."

"That would teach him," Wullie said with some pity.

"But know whit they did?" Annie went on with some awe.

"They shot the dug?" Wullie said.

Annie shook her head: "Naw, they took Wee Tommy's big toe aff his fit and sewed it on tae his haun. Know whit that meant tae the wee boy?"

"He was the only wean in the street wi' a verruca on his haun' ?" Wullie grinned.

"It meant he could use his haun' normally," Annie said.

"Ah never noticed," Wullie said, shaking his head, "ye could never tell, so ye couldnae. Ah never realised that when Ah saw him suckin' his thumb, he was really suckin' his toe. Aye, ye live an' learn!"

Annie turned on him: "Aye, well Ah wish you'd learn for tae get properly dressed when we have tae hurry doon tae the air-raid shelter," she sniped.

"Whit's wrang wi' the wey Ah dress?" Wullie said, peeved.

"Look at ye, " Annie snapped, "ye're like Wee Wullie Winkie. And another thing, ye do nut have tae cairry they wally dugs every time we dash doon. Gie me a showin' up!"

"They were OOR maw's," Wullie protested.

"That disnae matter. They were a weddin' present she got frae wan o' the stallholders at the Barras and she widnae like anythin' for to happen tae them. They could get damaged goin' up an' doon they stairs every time there's a raid." Annie was adamant.

"Whit if Ah ah'd left them an' the hoose got bombed, eh? Ah mean the Jerries have nae compunction. They don't care who or whit they bomb. The bomb drapper disnae look through his wee aimer an' say tae the pilot...'Go oan a bit further Adolph. That's Wullie McSorley's hoose doon there. Ah don't want for tae smash his wally dugs. His maw got them frae a man at the Barras.' That's no' how it works, Annie"

Annie shook her head despairingly "Och, ye talk rubbish at times, Wullie," she said. "Anywey, get yersel' a siren suit for heavens sake. Wan like Mr Churchill's."

Wullie's lips tightened. "Ah am nut goin' doon tae nae shelter lookin' like Mr Chrchill," he snapped. "Everybody would gie ME two fingers...and no' the same wey HE does it."

"Aw, Wullie!" was all that Annie said, glancing quickly upwards. "Ah don't think Ah'll even bother goin' doon tae the shelter again," Wullie said, "Ah mean, if yer name's oan it, yer name's oan it. An', besides, Ah'm fed up listenin' tae that wee nyaff on the mouth organ."

"Och, Wullie," Annie said in defence of the wee nyaff, "he's just tryin' tae cheer us up...take oor mind aff things... startin' a wee sing song."

"He's nothin' but a show aff!" Wullie said with some venom, "He thinks he's Larry Adler wi' a' that fancy playin'... a' that high falutin' stuff. 'Sing up', he shouts, 'Sing up'. Ah mean there's no' many people know the words o' Tchaikovsky's Fifth Symphony, Annie."

"He tries," Annie said.

"An' as for that sidekick o' his," Wullie went on with sarcasm, "staunin' there singin' away. Tryin tae sound like Deanna Durbin. It's pathetic!"

"A wonderful voice!" Annie said.

"No' for a man, Annie", Wullie replied, with a groan.

"He tries his best," Annie said, raising her voice.

"Ah'll tell ye this, Annie," Wullie went on, failing to note the anger welling up in his sister's voice, "either that bloke's got a serious mental problem or he has just returned frae Antartica."

Annie failed to see the connection and poured out two cups of tea.

"Here," she said, "there's nothin' tae beat a wee cup of tea."

"Oh aye there is," Wullie said with a twinkle.

They both sat in silence enjoying the warmth of the sweet tea.

"Ah wonder whit happened tae Ina?" Annie said at last. "She wisnae doon in the shelter. She probably slept through the sirens."

"Wise wumman!" Wullie commented.

"Still, it's dangerous," Annie said with a worried expression. "You should've went in an' pulled her oot her bed, Wullie."

Wullie spluttered in his tea.

"Are ye daft, Wumman?" he almost yelled. "If Ah had gone in there, she would've pulled me INTAE the bed."

Annie regretted Ina McLatchie's advances to Wullie had been spurned. She liked Ina and admired how she had looked after her ailing father in his old age. Wullie could not have found a more devoted wife and Annie had done all she could to encourage a romance. But Wullie never rose to the bait in Annie's wily schemes to be matchmaker although Annie was sure that her brother HAD a sneaking admiration for their next-door neighbour. But she knew, too, that he would never show it. She saw, too, the day that Ina might meet someone else and her wish for Wullie would die.

Turning on Wullie, she said: "Don't talk rubbish! You'd be so lucky that Ina would pull ye intae her bed. Ina McLatchie is wan o' the nicest lassies Ah know. And you should be ashamed o' yersel' the wey you've treated her. Ye led her on, that night in the air-raid shelter, so ye did. Ye did everythin' but propose."

Wullie shrugged, "Ah was shell shocked that night and, besides, Ah was nut gonny be bought by a couple o' soda scones."

Annie was now on her high horse. "Ye've let her doon at every turn," she said bitterly. "Even efter her faither's funeral. The lassie asked ye tae collect his ashes and even in that ye let her doon."

"It wisnae ma fault Ah accidently flushed them doon the sink at the pub, so it wisnae." he said sulkily.

"Ye shouldnae have been anywhere near a pub cairryin' that auld man's ashes," Annie said angrily.

"Ah was thirsty an' Ah jist went in for a pint an' Ah laid the ashes on tap o' the bar and the barman's dug knocked it intae the sink while the well was runnin'. So, it was the dug's fault, no' mine."

But Annie was not going to let him off the hook.

"THAT was bad enough," she snapped, " But tae fill up a pint tumbler wi' soot and present it tae Ina pretendin' it was her faither.. THAT was sacrilege so it was. Then, on toap o' that, tae sprinkle the ashes on the winbdae boax an' say a prayer ower them..."

"Well, Ah thought Ah was daein' the right thing," Wullie said with a hint of contrition.

"Ah'll tell ye this, Wullie," Annie went on, "if you don't grab Ina while the goin's good, you'll be sorry, Ah'm tellin' ye."

Maybe Annie was right, Wullie thought. But he was not ready for marriage. He enjoyed too much the freedom of bachelorhood. Annie looked after him like no wife could, he reckoned. And he loved going down to the Well Street corner and chatting to the 'Coarner Boys' who hung around outside

11

the Calton Social Club every day. Afterwards he would cross Stevenston Street and spend an hour or two having a few pints in the Come Inn Pub and a 'blether' with Jimmy Smith the barman. Other times, at the weekends, he would saunter round 'The Barras' where you could buy anything from an out of date Harry Lauder gramophone record to a battleship...or so it seemed. Yes, Wullie loved his freedom and all Annie's cajoling would make no difference. Looking up at Annie, he said:

"It's the thought of listenin' tae Ina talkin' aboot her faither a' day. Of how great an actor he was. Of how he took her tae Hollywood wance and she was introduced tae Rin-Tin-Tin, the great dug actor. She never stoaps talkin' aboot it. It would drive me roon' the bend. Tae think the greatest moment of yer life is bein' introduced tae a dug. If she had met Errol Flynn or somebody like that, then she would have somethin' tae shout aboot," he added sourly.

"If she'd met Errol Flynn she'd never have looked at you," Annie said facetiously, adding, "In fact even efter meetin' the dug Ah'm surprised she even fancied you."

Wullie took umbrage at that remark.

"Hhmph!" he said, "You've a cheek tae talk. Look whit you ended up wi'... SAMMY."

Annie did not like anyone decrying her Sammy. Her back up, she snapped, "The minute Ah saw Sammy wi' his teeth in Ah knew he was mine."

"Are ye sure the teeth wurnae yours?" Wullie sniped, "Ah mean your Sammy has been known for tae have torry fingers."

"That's a lie," Annie snapped. "The only thing ma Sammy ever stole was a kiss."

"An' that's probably when he stole yer teeth!" Wullie exclaimed. "Wan big suck wull dae it! But this has got nothin' tae dae wi' you tryin' for tae mairry me aff."

"Ye're no' gettin' any younger, Wullie," Annie retorted. "Marriage is a great institution. There's oor Rita noo. Her an' Rasputin are livin' in bliss."

"They'd rather be livin' in a hoose," Wullie said snidely.

Wullie was right Annie thought. Getting a house was no easy matter. Applying to the Glasgow Corporation was wasted effort and, unless you knew a factor, or, more importantly, a factor who took 'bungs' young couples had to rely on the good hospitality of their parents or friends. And even if they WERE lucky to acquire keys for a house the chances were that their dream home would be a 'single-end'...one room with a bed recess and a lavatory outside on the stair landing to be shared with the other tenants on the landing. An indoor toilet was out of the question.

A room and kitchen was Shangri La and to acquire one was akin to winning the Grand National. And, while some couples DID manage to walk into a room and kitchen talk would be that they must have given a good 'bung' or, in the case of the Catholics, their Novena to the Blessed Virgin was answered.

"Where is Rita anywey?" Wullie said with a frown and just realising his wee niece was not with them when they hurried to the shelter.

"She's was steyin' the night wi' Wee Maisie McLaughlin last night. They were goin' straight oot tae Barraland when they finished their shifts at the depot," Annie said quite unconcerned. Her reasoning being that, although Rita was now a married woman, the trauma of war allowed her daughter to take what relaxation she could. For working on the Glasgow 'Caurs' brought its own traumas and she knew, too, that Rita would never be led astray by the charms of any other man... even the a charming Texan drawl from a homesick G.I.

"She's as happy as Larry," she added, making sure that Wullie did not get the wrong ideas.

"No' Larry Adler Ah hope," Wullie grinned.

"It's just an expression," Annie said, as though an explanation was necessary. "She just lives for the day when Rasputin comes hame."

Wullie smiled, "And whit aboot Sammy?" he asked, showing interest. "Where is he noo since his escape frae that Japanese prison camp on that Pacific island?"

Annie clasped her hands together and gazed skywards.

"Oh ma Sammy!" she said proudly. "It says a loat for him escapin' and fighin' his wey through that jungle for days an' months, swimmin as fast as he could through they shark-infested watters of the Pacific Ocean. He didnae hauf gie that

American sojer a fright as he staggered oot the inky blackness collapsing in his erms."

"He didnae half," Wullie sniped, "that sojer was staunin' on a platform on a San Francisco station waitin' for a subway."

"Sammy always was a strong swimmer," Annie said with pride.

"Whit's he daein' noo?" Wullie asked.

"When he got back tae his camp, in Catterick, he was paraded before the whole regiment and the general himsel' promoted him.. tae private."

"If he swims the Atlantic they might gie him a stripe," Wullie said sarcastically.

Before Annie could reply the door flew open and Ina McLatchie came hurrying in shouting.

"Annie...oh, Annie...!"

Annie and Wullie jumped to their feet and Ina flopped down breathlessly on Annie's vacant seat. She held her clenched fist to her chest and took deep breaths.

"Oh, Annie!" she repeated.

"Whi... whit is it? Whit is it, Ina?" Annie said, finding herself panicking.

Ina could barely catch her breath. She was obviously distressed. Annie put a comforting arm around her shoulder.

"C'mon, hen, whit is it?" she said softly.

Ina took a deep breath.

"It.. it's ma da'," she said.

"Don't tell me he's sprouted up oot the windae boax?" Wullie said sarcastically

"He.. he.. appeared tae me," Ina said, now calmed down.

"APPEARED TAE YE?" Wullie and Annie said in unison.

Ina nodded. She dabbed her eyes with a handkerchief.

"Aye," she said, "Ah woke up wi' the sirens wailin'...an' there he was...staunin' at the foot o' ma bed. Just staunin' there...STARIN' Ah sat up wi' a start...Ah got such a fright."

"Seein' you, it's a wonder HE didnae get a fright," Wullie said impishly.

Ina ignored the facetious remark.

"He just stood there," she said, almost in awe, "bathed in a beautiful light."

14

"He always DID have a good glow oan," Wullie volunteered.

"Did he say whit he wanted, Ina?" Annie quietly asked.

"He was probably lookin' for the lavvy," Wullie said. "He was always lookin' for the lavvy."

Annie glared at him.

"He just stood there," Ina went on as though in a dream, "just starin' at me...STARIN'."

"A loat o' people dae that when they see you," Wullie said.

Annie threw him a glance that would sink the Tirpitz.

"Ma haun' came up tae ma mooth," Ina said.

"Ye should get gum that would haud ye teeth in," Wullie suggested.

"He must've had a message for ye," Annie said, adding, "did he have wings?"

"He disnae need wings," Wullie said, "he was always fleein'."

Ina shook her head.

"Naw nae wings," she said, "just a halo above his heid."

"Probably a noose," Wullie said.

"Did he say anythin' aboot his funeral?" Annie asked, thinking about the calamitous handling of old Jake's departure by Wullie.

"No' really," Ina said, "he always believed aboot out of body experiences."

"So he should," Wullie said, "he was always oot his skull."

Annie sent another torpedo his way, "WULLIE!" she rebuked loudly, adding, "Go on, Ina, Ah know exactly whit ye mean. That's when ye get that feelin' like ye're rushin' doon a daurk tunnel wi' a light at the end o' it. And, when ye come oot the tunnel intae the light ye find yersel' in Heaven... wonderful!"

He says he found himsel' rushin' doon the tunnel wi' a sound like rushin' watter. At he end o' the tunnel he could see the brilliant light an' he couldnae wait tae get there and when he DID come oot intae the light he was disappointed no' tae find himsel' in Heaven," Ina panted.

"Oh, don't tell me," Annie wailed, "he...he...wisnae in the other place, was he? I...He... Hell!" she stammered.

"Naw, he was in Rothesay," Ina said.

15

Annie immediately scowled at Wullie.

"That long tunnel was the Come Inn's waste pipe," Annie said angrily.

"Blame Dougal, the dug," Wullie shrugged.

Ina smiled, "Ma faither was dressed as King Lear," she said proudly.

"Why not? He was the biggest leer in the street," Wullie sniped.

"Did he say anythin' else, hen?" Annie prodded.

"Aye, he says your Sammy's gonny get drapped ower France again," Ina said.

"Aw, naw!" Annie wailed.

Wullie put an arm around Annie's shoulder.

"Never mind, Annie," he said "they'll probably gie him a parachute this time."

Annie ignored Wullie's sarcasm.

"Whit else, Ina?"

Ina sighed. "He says Ah'll soon be gettin' a ring," she said.

"You hivnae got a phone," Wullie piped up.

"An' Ah'll be walkin' doon the aisle all aglow an' happy," Ina said dreamily.

"Probably walkin' backwards aglow wi' the ice-cream tray ye're cairryin'. Yer gettin' a joab as an usherette in the Arcadia, that's whit it is," Wullie said without a smile.

But Ina was not listening. She was thinking of the rest of her dead father's message.

"He said that he could see a man in uniform — a WHITE uniform — lookin' intae ma eyes."

Annie clapped her hands together.

"Oh, maybe it's a naval officer in his tropical uniform. How excitin'!"

"Aw, he looked the picture o' health," Ina said happily.

"He's bloody deid," Wullie bawled.

"Well, he looked that happy." Ina went on, "He said he'd met many auld freen's frae Hollywood...Rin-Tin-Tin amongst others."

"Was the dug alang wi' him?" Wullie asked, knitting his brows.

Ina shook her head.

16

"Naw," she said, "the dug wisnae wi' him. Whit makes ye ask?"

"That landin' oot there was full o' crap when we hurried doon tae the shelter. Ah nearly went oan ma neck."

"It wisnae Rin-Tin-Tin," Ina said sternly.

"A'right, Ah staun' corrected," Wullie said. "In that case it must've been Auld Shug frae up the stairs. It's funny oor landin' seems tae get it durin' an air raid. Ah was blamin' that snarlin' dug that's been frequentin' oor close recently. Ah had tried tae make freens wi' it. But when Ah went near it, it growled and showed me it's teeth."

"It's the war," Annie, a dog lover, said in mitigation. It's they sirens that terrify even the maist docile dugs. They're that terrified that even the usually friendly dug shows ye its teeth when approached." Wullie shook his head vehemently.

"No' like this dug did," he said "...an alsatian, it is."

"So, whit was so special aboot it?" Annie quizzed.

"It took them oot an' showed me them," Wullie said.

"Och, don't talk rubbish," Annie said with a dismissive wave. "Don't listen tae him, Ina. Noo, aboot yer faither, did he say anythin' else?"

Ina sighed once more, "He said he could see me walkin' doon the aisle, ma 'groom, in uniform staunin' waitin' by the altar waitin' for me. He said Ah'd be cairryin' a horse shoe."

"Wi' your build you could cairry the hoarse," Wullie said cheekily.

Ina let that go by. She was used to Wullie's snipes now and tried to ignore them completely.

"Anythin' else?" Annie asked excitedly.

"Ah'd have somethin' coverin' ma face," Ina said.

"A bag?" Wullie asked.

"A VEIL?" Ina snapped.

Annie glowered at Wullie.

"See," she snapped, "Ah telt ye!"

Ina's mind was dreamily racing.

"Ma da' says the man in the white uniform would click his heels an' salute me. Oh, it's that excitin'."

"Sounds like a bloody German tae me! "Wullie growled.

Annie gave Ina's shoulders a tender squeeze.

"Ye're due some happiness, hen!" she said, scowling at Wullie.

Reading Annie's thoughts, Wullie clapped his hands together. "Aye," he said, "well, when Ah decide for tae take a wife she'll have tae look like ma ideal wumman"

An' who's yer ideal wumman?" Annie asked, raising her eyebrows.

"Mae West," Wullie said with a smug expression.

"MAE WEST?" Annie hollered, laughing. "Listen, Wullie, if Cary Grant couldnae get her, you hiv nae chance."

Wullie dismissed Annie's comment with a rasping sound.

Walking over to the wireless, he switched it on.

"Ach, let's have some music tae cheers us up."

But no music came from the speaker. Instead the dull monotone of Lord Haw Haw, the German propaganda broadcaster flooded the room.

"Och, no' HIM," Annie moaned. "Switch him aff."

"Naw, leave him on. He gies us a laugh," Wullie said.

"GERMANY CALLING...GERMANY CALLING," the boring, flat voice began.

"Y'know, that bloke knows everythin' that's goin' on in Glesca, so he does. It's uncanny, so it is," Annie said.

Wullie shook his head.

"Naw, naw," he said with knowledge, "ye just think that. They're experts at it. They can make ye believe anythin' they want... Just let it go in wan ear an' oot the other...noo listen."

The wireless voice droned on.

"And now a special word for you Glesca Keelies. I see that Gone with The Wind is still on at the Paramount, in Renfield Street. and Billy McGregor and his Gaybirds Dance Band is still packing them in at Barrowland or, should I say, Barraland, to use the vernacular?

And how about YOU, Wullie McSorley of twenty-seven Well Street, in the Calton, eh? What about that clever dog that showed you it's teeth, eh? A well trained dog, that, eh? And why not! After all, Willie, it WAS a GERMAN shepherd."

Steam jetted out of Wullie's ears.

"How did he know that?" he screamed. "There is only wan explanation."

"Ah telt ye," Annie said smugly, "wa's have ears!"

"Naw, naw, there's a traitor up this close...a spy. Ah'll kill him, so Ah wull. Ah'll no' be able tae show ma face in the Calton efter his scurrilous guff."

"Never tae enter the Come Inn Pub again, Wullie," Annie said.

"Naw, naw, things urnae as bad as that, Annie," Wullie said quickly, adding, "And he was wrang. That dug was nae German. Its bark was nae different frae any normal Glesca dug. But HOW DID HE KNOW ABOOT THAT EPISODE? Somebody is gien' secrets away...and there's only wan man up this close that can be daein' that!"

"An' who's that?" Ina asked, wide-eyed.

"Your bloody faither," Wullie snapped.

"Ma da'?" Ina said, her mouth falling open.

"Yiour faither is appearin' tae Hitler an' tellin' him everythin' that's goin' oan. He is tellin' him oor secrets. He is the only wan that can flit aboot withoot a passport."

"Ach, don't talk rubbish!" Annie said contemptuously.

"Rubbish, is it?" Wullie snapped. "Ah'm tellin' ye, Ah was always suspicious aboot auld McLatchie. Ah knew there was somethin' aboot him Ah didnae like."

"Ma faither was a gentleman, a great actor," Ina protested.

"Naw, naw, that's the impression he gave," Wullie cried. "Secretly he had German sympathies. Ah should've known that day Ah was walkin' up the close and saw that terrible face wi' a Hitler moustache comin' doon the stairs."

"That was ma da'?" Ina said incredulously.

"It was yer maw," Wullie sniped.

Annie felt the anger swelling up inside her. "Don't talk such rubbish," she stormed. "Ina's maw was a fine lookin' wumman."

"No' wi' that moustache she wisnae," Wullie snapped. "Auld Jake wanted a' his faimly tae resemble Hitler. It was when he turned tae the cat that Ah objected.."

Ina was furious. "Ur you suggestin' that ma da' stuck a Hitler moustache on oor cat?" she cried.

"Ah am," Wullie said without blinking.

"Whit nonsense!" Ina said. "Every cat's got whiskers."

"No' shaped like a penny-black stamp, they don't, Wullie said. "And did ye never notice that yer cat was reluctant tae go oot at night... like a' other normal cats dae?"

"That's no' true," Ina said, holding back a tear.

"Oh, aye, it's true a'right," Wullie said smugly. "It didnae go oot 'cos every cat in the street was waitin' for it tae gie it a tankin'. They used tae call it 'Mein Herr' and, by the time they were finished wi' it, they called it 'Nae Hair'."

All were startled as the door burst open and Rita, still in uniform, hurried in.

"Oh, Mammy," she cried, "Ah was worried when Ah heard the air raid."

Annie was pleased that her daughter had thought about her. She gave Rita's arm a tender squeeze.

"Naw, we're a'right, hen. Ah thought you were goin' straight tae Barraland efter ye finished yer shift?"

Rita flopped on to a chair. "Wee Maisie and me DID go tae Barraland and then went back tae Maisie's hoose in Fairbairn Street. Ah was sound asleep when the sirens went. Ah just had tae come hame efter the All Clear tae see you were a'right."

Annie pecked Rita's cheek. "Aw, that was awfu' thoughtful o' ye, hen," she said almost in a whisper. "But we're a' a'right.... jist Ina there had a frightenin' experience."

"Oh! Whit happened, Ina?" Rita asked with concern.

"Her faither appeared tae her from his celestial home," Annie volunteered.

"He was in spirit form," Ina added, dabbing her eyes and sobbing quietly.

Wullie grunted, "He was ALWAYS in spirit form, the auld drunk," he said.

Ina turned on him, "Ur you suggestin' that ma faither had a drinkin' problem?" she snapped, adding, between sobs, "he was a very modest drinker — a hauf pint a day."

"Aye, a hauf pint o' Johnny Walker," Wullie sniped.

Annie stepped in quickly to avoid any further confrontation between Ina and Wullie.

"Did he...er...say anythin' else, yer da'?" she said. "Like, for instance, when this war is gonny end?"

Ina shook her head.

20

"Naw," she said. "Before Ah could ask him anythin' else he jist turned intae a kinda vapour...like steam."

Wullie nodded. "That would be aboot right," he said, "he was always steamin'!"

"He DID say Ah was gonny walk doon the aisle," she said with a cheerier note

"Backwards," Wullie added.

Rita affectionately squeezed Ina's shoulder and kissed her cheek.

"Oh, that's lovely, Ina," she twittered. "Who's the lucky man?"

Ina shook her head. "Ah've nae idea," she said.

"Ah know who it isnae," Wullie added.

"HE fancies Mae West," Annie scoffed.

Rita laughed. "Some, hope!" she said.

"But whit aboot Rasputin?" Ina asked, turning the attention away from herself.

Rita sighed, "Oh, don't mention it," she said, "The last letter Ah got said he was goin' on a dangerous mission. He said he couldnae tell me wheraboots he was aff tae as it was classified."

"He should be certified, " Wullie said dryly.

"So, ye've nae idea where he's goin'?" Ina asked.

Rita shook her head, "Naw, he said he couldnae tell me," she said sadly, "But he said he'd be thinkin' of me and that he would be singin' oor ain special song in his heart as he goes intae danger." Rita spoke as though in a dream. She went on, "He said, 'Ah'll be singin' oor ain song, darlin' — the wan Ah sing tae ye when Ah hold you in ma erms and look intae yer lovely eyes."

"Aw, how romantic!" Ina gasped, clasping her heart.

"Whit song is that, then?" Annie asked.

Rita sighed once more, "Ye canny shove yer granny aff a bus," she said almost in a dreamy whisper.

Wullie's brows shot up, "He canny be goin' that faur intae danger if THAT'S the clue," he sneered.

"Whit dae ye mean?" Rita snapped, knowing full well that they wouldn't be sending her Rasputin into anything that was not fraught with danger.

Wullie shrugged, "Well, normally when they send these blokes on dangerous missions intae enemy territory, they drap them by parachute or they go by submarine and paddle ashore in a dinghy. They don't usually say, 'Right, away youse go...get the number fifty-two bus at the coarner."

Ina pooh-poohed Wullie's thesis.

"Away ye go!" she said contemptuously, "Ah'm sure Rasputin didnae mean THAT. Did he say anythin' else, Rita?"

"He just said he wished he could tell me where was goin'... that he could be mair frank...but he spelt frank, F-R-A-N-C."

Wullie slapped his thigh.

"That's it then, intit," he cried. "That's the clue... the letter 'C'. It's obvious where he's bein' sent." Wullie grinned, pleased with himself.

"Oh, where, Uncle Wullie?" Rita cried.

"China," Wullie replied smugly.

"How dae ye make that oot?" Annie said, narrowing her eyes.

"'C' - for China... get it?" Wullie said cockily.

"Ah've never heard such tripe in ma life!" Annie exclaimed.

"Ah would hazard a guess that he means France where the franc is the currency."

"That sounds mair like it," Ina agreed.

"Here, maybe he'll meet Big Sammy ower there," Annie piped up.

Wullie shook his head.

"It's highly unlikely," he said.

"Oh, Ah don't know," Annie said, "Rasputin might just walk intae a bistro wan day and there's Sammy staunin' there."

"Naw, naw, " Wullie said, shaking his head. "Sammy would never frequent a bistro...he's an Oxo man."

Annie, despairingly, threw her eyes skywards.

"Wouldn't it be strange if they were oan the same mission?" she cried. "Blawin' up bridges an' that!"

"It takes Sammy a' his time tae blaw his nose," Wullie sniped. "If he was a red Indian he'd be called Big Chief Runnin' Conk!"

Annie ignored Wullie's sarcasm. "Aw, if only this war would end and we could a' get back tae normal." She sighed deeply.

Everyone fell silent. Rita thought of Rasputin, wondering what dangers he faced and if she should ever see him again? She thought of happier times. Of her wedding and of how her mother had worried about the catering. Her mother, bless her, had her own worries.

She remembered how Fingers McGeachie had come to the rescue by acquiring a whole pig....only to lose it as Special Constable, Erchie McPherson, closed in and the pig had to be disposed of quickly... Of how the Luftwaffe came to her aid by supplying her wedding dress. That was another capture for Erchie McPherson when he proudly arrested a shot-down German pilot who had baled out and was caught hiding in the back-court wash House at 27, Well Street. The retrieved silk parachute was quickly transformed by expert seamstress, Mrs Cominsky, who lived up the next close. Everything had gone smoothly until Rasputin received his Calling-Up papers and was whisked into the army. Already he had given his plans for ending the war to the War Office and Rita was extremely proud of him. Now she was worrying.

Annie, too, was worried. She was over the moon when Sammy escaped from the Japanese Prisoner of War Camp. Now he was home and was being thrown into more danger. She looked at Ina and whether Ina had imagined her father's vision it didn't matter. Ina was happy. She saw herself being married at last. Annie was only sorry that Wullie had never shown more interest in Ina and had rebuffed her advances. Perhaps she had made things too comfortable for her brother! Although she had a sneaking feeling that Wullie did carry a torch for Ina, albeit a flickering flame deep down somewhere in the corner of his heart. But Wullie would never admit it. Perhaps it wasn't too late !

TWO

FINGERS MCGEACHIE'S NAME WAS WHISPERED WITH REVERENCE. To the old folk he was the saint of the Calton. Saint Fingers was always there when a bit of extra butter was needed, or a pound of sugar or bacon. Yes, Fingers was a rogue but a likeable one. Only one man thought of Fingers McGeachie with gritted teeth. Special Constable Erchie McPherson had two missions in life. His first was be allowed into the regular Glasgow City Police Force. But his five-foot six inch stature had barred him from this exalted post. His other was to nail Fingers McGeachie. The fact that Fingers was revered as a Robin Hood of the tenements did not matter. The law was the law and He, Erchie, would uphold it to the best of his ability. He had come close to getting Fingers but had never quite made it. This had made him more determined. He had almost caught him after Fingers had dumped the wedding pig in Annie's house but Wullie had managed to chuck it out of the window in the nick of time. He nearly captured him, too, when he found Fingers pushing a barrowload of illicit booze. But Fingers had a guardian angel and a silver tongue. Rita's catering problem was finally settled when jovial Big Mario Valente who had the local chip shop, turned up on the wedding day at the eleventh hour with a basketful of succulent fish suppers. Mario had saved the day! Mario had been exempt from a British prison camp. In June 1940 scores of Italians living in Glasgow where interred by the government. Many were freed later and proudly displayed in the window of Mario's chip shop, in London Road, was a printed notice saying, "I have two sons serving with the British Army."

Mario was proud of Scotland and Glasgow was proud of Mario...especially Annie on that fateful wedding day.

The door opened and Special Constable Erchie McPherson

dashed, breathlessly, in. He made straight for the window and adjusted the blackout curtain.

"Wan chink o' light can be seen at ten thousand feet," he gasped.

"Ah'm fed up wi' ye tellin' us that," Annie said. "Aye, and besides, the All-Clear's gone. They're away hame tae get stuck intae their schnapps." she added.

"Don't be so sure, Annie," Wullie said. "That might've just been the first wave. There could be mair tae come. Ye canny be too careful!"

Erchie suddenly noticed Ina was in the company.

"Oh, hello, Ina," he said, "Ah didnae recognise ye there! It's a'right, hen, the Jerries are away. Nae need for tae keep yer gas mask on."

Ina drew herself up, "Ah am nut wearin' ma gas mask," she blurted.

"Oh, sorry," Erchie said.

"Ye should wear it," Wullie said, "It would be an improvement." Annie kicked Wullie on the ankle with a strong rebuke.

"WULLIE!"

Wullie groaned and rubbed his ankle, throwing a scowl at Annie.

"Ye're lookin' lovely the night, Annie," Erchie said. "It's the first time Ah've seen ye in yer night attire!"

"Aye, and it'll be the last," Annie retorted. She knew Erchie liked her but she was true to Big Sammy. Her 'man' was away fighting for his country and she would be there waiting patiently until his return. She would be faithful to the end and pompous Erchie was nowhere in her heart.

"Ye're oot a bit late, ur ye no', Erchie?" Wullie piped in.

"We are always on the job, Wullie," Erchie said, putting his arms behind him and stretching to his full height. "We never sleep. We are oot there daein' oor duty for King and country. The Luftwaffe wull never get ME doon!" he gave a smart click of the tongue.

"Me neither," Ina added.

"Well, maybe no' the whole squadron, Ina," Wullie said sarcastically.

Ina ignored his remark.

"Well, at least wan good thing has come oot o' this war", Erchie said.

"And whit's that?" Annie asked, puzzled.

Erchie gave a slight cough. "Well," he said, "because Ah captured that German pilot, the Chief Constable, Mr Percy Sillitoe hisel', has hinted that he might waive a' height restrictions in ma case for to join the regular polis force."

"Aw, that's wonderful, Erchie," Annie cried.

"Geez, they'll be recruitin' Snow White next," Wullie said snidely.

It gave Erchie a great kick announcing his hopeful acceptance into the Glasgow City Police. His height had maybe stayed the same but he went up in stature.

"Aye, ye can always depend on me, Annie," he said proudly, "Ah'll always be there for to protect ye... even if Big Sammy disnae come back."

Wullie shook his head. He was thinking that things in the City police force must be desperate if they were considering taking Erchie into their ranks. In wartime everything was desperate, but he still could not hold back his sarcasm.

"Aye, Ah can just see it noo," he said. "Hitler must be shakin' in his shoes. Ah can just see him throwin' up his erms and, in sheer despair and wi' tears runnin' oot his eyes, bawlin', 'That's it! The war is ower...we've loast a' because of that swinehund Erchie McPherson...'"

"Aye, Wullie you can laugh!" Annie said.

"Ye've got tae!" Wullie replied.

Erchie bit his lip. "There's wan mair thorn in ma side Ah would've like for to have been extracated before hingin' up ma special tin helmet," he said.

"Oh! An' whit's that, Erchie?" Annie asked, raising her eyebrows.

"Ah would have loved for to have nailed Fingers McGeachie," Erchie said with some bitterness.

Wullie couldn't hold back the laugh that came from him, "Ye'll need tae be smart tae get the finger on Fingers," he chuckled.

"Aye, well, we'll see," Erchie said, hurt that his ability was being questioned.

Annie quickly stepped in to steer the conversation away from Erchie's prowess.

"Erchie, did ye know that Wullie was mentioned oan the wireless this mornin'?"

"AH have nae time for listenin' tae the wireless durin' enemy raids," Erchie said pompously. "Ah have other things oan ma mind...saving people an' that. The only wireless Ah listen in tae is the Polis wave band wot gives me expert instructions like where tae make for to save people an' that."

"Aye, well, we a' know that, Erchie," Annie said. " But Wullie WAS mentioned oan the wireless."

Erchie raised his eyebrows.

"Oh!" he exclaimed, "An' who mentioned him? George Elrick, in Housewives Choice?"

"Naw, don't be daft," Annie said. "It's too early for that. Naw, it wisnae George Elrick or even Wilfred Pickles. But somebody just as famous."

"An' who might that be?" Erchie said, intrigued.

"Lord Haw Haw," Wullie interrupted, with a slight puff of the chest.

Erchie spluttered.

"LORD HAW HAW? LORD HAW HAW?" he hollered.

"Aye, "Annie said. "He knew a' aboot a confrontation he had wi' a dug."

"An' Ah want tae know how HE knew aboot it? There's only wan possible explanation."

"Whit's that?" Erchie asked, becoming more intrigued.

"There's a spy up this close." Wullie said, tightening his lips.

"A SPY?" Erchie yelled, his ears pricking up.

"Aye, a traitor," Wullie went on. "And Ah know who it is. It was her faither." Wullie spun round and pointed a finger at Ina.

Erchie burst out laughing. "Ah, rubbish! Auld Jake's deid," he chortled. "You've been on the jungle juice again, Wullie," he said.

Wullie took umbrage at that. "Is that so?" he snapped. "Well it's obvious that you are unaware that her da's ghost is appearin' a' ower the place. It is ma contention that he has just returned frae Berlin where he has been haudin' conversations

27

wi wan Herr Hitler and gien's said Herr oor deepest secrets."

Wullie felt better getting it off his chest.

"And you think that tellin' Lord Haw Haw that you had an altercation wi' a dug comes under the head o' wan oor deepest secrets, eh? "

"Who else has free access for tae move aboot?" Wullie said.

"Maybe the dug sent him a letter," Erchie chortled.

"Aye, well laugh if ye like," Wullie said, "but Ah know whit Ah think."

Ina was getting angrier listening to this conversation about her dear father.

"Ma da' was nae traitor," she snapped. "He would never dae such a thing, alive OR deid, so he widnae. He fought in the Crimea."

"There's always fights in that wee picture hall," Wullie volunteered.

"Whit are ye talkin' aboot?" Ina snarled.

"The Crimea...that wee picture hall in Toonheid."

"Away ya ignorant get!" Ina sniped. "Ah'm talkin' aboot the Crimea...Ye've heard o' the Charge of the Light Brigade? Balaclava?"

"Ah never wear them," Wullie said, running his hand over his thinning hair.

"There's nae talkin' tae you," Ina said, dumped.

"Ye can talk tae me if ye like...but that's a'?" Wullie said. "It does nut detract frae the fact that your faither had nazi sympathies."

"Whit makes ye say that, Wullie?" Erchie asked, narrowing his eyes.

"'Cos he had a' his faimily indoctrinated. He wanted them a' tae resemble the Fuehrer...even his cat stuck up it's front paw when ye passed it. That cat was brainwashed."

"Wee Adolph? AH don't believe it," Erchie said.

"OOR cat was nut called Adolph," Ina protested.

"Whit was it called, then?" Wullie questioned

"Herman," Ina said innocently.

Wullie smacked his hands together. "Ah-Ha," he yelled. "There ye are, then — Herman the German, Ah telt youse."

Ina was not pleased at the tenor of this conversation. "Ma

faither was a true patriot," she snapped. "He wance played Bonnie Prince Charlie."

Wullie threw up his hands. "Whit a case of mis-castin', " he said. "Ah mean, Quasimodo was an Errol Flynn look-alike compared tae your auld man...no' tae mention yer maw."

Annie saw the despair on Ina's face. She was taking a lot of banter from Wullie and Annie was getting angry. It should be the other way round to her mind. Wullie and Ina should be holding hands, gazing into each others eyes and whispering sweet nothings. It seemed to her that Wullie was going out of his way to be extremely rude. She wondered why. Could it be that he did not like the prediction of Ina walking down the aisle with an unknown stranger? Was Wullie jealous?

Annie put an arm around Ina's shoulder. "Don't let HIM rile ye, Ina," she said, throwing darts at Wullie. "Just think whit's ahead...walking doon the aisle. The handsome man in a white uniform...."

"Naebody said he was handsome," Wullie interrupted, "...or even that he'd be walkin' doon that aisle..."

"Well, anywey, it a' sounds lovely, hen." Annie smiled.

Annie's outburst sent Ina dreaming.

"Aye, maybe an officer...a' in white," she sighed and let her mind race though all the handsome men she admired — Errol Flynn, Ronald Coleman -Tyrone Power - Robert Taylor. They were all there standing at the foot of the aisle, dazzling teeth blinding in the sunlight beaming through the window, dressed in brilliant white uniforms and with crooked arm and all looking at HER coming down the aisle. All waiting for HER. Ina sighed deeply.

Annie brought her back to reality. "Aye, Ina," she said, "your day wull come. It's never too late tae find happiness!"

Turning to Wullie she added. "That right, Wullie?"

Wullie shrugged. What was his sister trying to get him involved in? He said nothing.

Annie looked at Ina who was thinking of things to come.

"Is there anythin' ye've ever regretted in yer life up till noo, Ina?" she said.

"Forby no' gettin' a man?" Wullie added, ignoring the glare from Annie.

Ina put a forefinger up to her cheek and thought. "Aye, as a matter of fact there is?" she said. "It sounds daft but when Ah was a wee lassie Ah got ma ears pierced an' ma da' bought be a pair o' cheap earrings. Well, Ah thought they were lovely. They looked just like real diamonds. Ah think he peyed a tanner for them. Anywey, efter a while Ah got a bad infection on ma ears and ma faither was beside himsel'."

"Geez, no' two o' him! Wan's bad enough", Wullie blurted.

Ina ignored him and carried on. "Anywey, he swore that wan day he would buy me a pair o' good earrings — wans wi' real diamonds. But he never did. They earrings were ma dearest wish but Ah never got them."

"Aw!" Annie said, "Whit a shame!"

"Ah still dream aboot them earrings Ah never got.."

"How's yer infection?" Wullie asked.

"Ah telt ye, Ah was just a wee lassie at the time. Ma infection vanished...just like ma dream," Ina said sadly.

Annie felt a lump in her throat. She, too, knew how it was to be a disappointed child. She and Wullie were brought up in the tenements and poverty ruled. Even grown up they came through the Depression Years of the late Twenties and Thirties. They saw and heard the backcourt singers. With shakey barrows they raided the coal reas to bring home coal lumps for the bunker inside the house and for the black-leaded range. They watched their father, in ragged jacket, head for the 'Broo' every week to collect their life for another miserable week. They saw their mother take a 'caur' to Milngavie where she did a bit of cleaning for a doctor and his wife. And she was glad of the work. It was only when war with Germany loomed that the gears of industry began to turn. Some factories changed their production methods. Famous furniture manufacturers, H. Morris and Company, of Wilton Street, set up a factory at Campsie and began turning out helicopter blades and Enfield rifles and other war materials. Her parents were long gone now but Annie remembered how the poverty spilled over to her early married years to Big Sammy. They struggled but they were not alone. Everybody was in the same boat and that allowed their dignity to stay put. Diamond earrings would only be seen on the delicate ears of Greta Garbo or

Gloria Swanson, the film goddesses. Ina seemed to read Annie's thoughts.

"Because ma da' worked in Hollywood he never made enough money tae buy me they earrings," she said in way of mitigation.

"Ye would think that bein' a film star ye'd make a loat o' money," Annie suggested.

"Believe me, Annie, Rin-Tin-Tin earned mair money than ma faither so it did," Ina said with some bitterness.

Wullie was about to challenge Ina's last statement when a loud rapping at the door made everyone jump.

"Ah'll get it," Annie said hurrying over. A muffled conversation was heard in the lobby before Annie entered followed by the milkman.

"Hello," the milkman smiled, "Ah'm Charlie Gallagher, yer new milkman." Ina's eyes popped as did Annie's.

Charlie Gallagher stood erect as a Guards officer. He wore a brilliantly white uniform with a skipped hat, whose brim shone like ebony. He clicked his heels and saluted smartly.

"Where's Wee Shuggie, oor regular man?" Rita said.

"He has taken the King's shullin'," Charlie said. "Ah am his replacement. Ah was hopin' for to be a Fighter Pilot but Ah failed the medical. They widnae even take me intae the caterin' corps."

"Aw, whit a shame!" Annie commiserated. "Still, looki at the lovely uniform they gied ye...A lovely WHITE uniform, eh, Ina?"

Ina blushed, "Beautiful!" she said.

Charlie turned to Ina, "Thanks, missus," he said, flashing a polished ivory smile.

"MISS," Ina corrected.

"You're no' the lovely Ina McLatchie Ah've been hearin' aboot, ur ye?"

Ina giggled and Wullie immediately piped up, "Was it yer bad eyesight that made ye fail yer medical?" he said sourly

Charlie didn't bother to answer Wullie's snide question. Turning to Ina, he said, "Yer faither was a famous actor, that right?"

"Aye, he played wi' Rin-Tin-Tin," Ina said proudly.

31

"Who's that?" Charlie asked, narrowing his eyes.

"A dug," Wullie said, "who, it seems, was a better actor than her da'...better peyed anyway."

Charlie pressed on, "Well," he said, taking Ina's hand, "Ah think you could've been a film star, Miss McLatchie...another Betty Grable! You're lovely!"

Ina blushed. "Coo!!!" she twittered, patting her hair at the back of her head.

"Whit.. er.. kinda dug was this Can-Tin-Can?" Charlie said, adding, "Ah used tae train dugs. Me an ma wee pal Two Fingers Gibson."

"That's a strange name, Two Fingers," Annie volunteered.

"Aye, well his real name was Horace, right enough," Charlie said.

"He's better stickin' tae Two Fingers," Wullie piped in.

"Aye, well, he had the bad habit o' stickin' his haun inside a dug's mooth and wan by wan his fingers disappeared till he was left wi' just two and that's how he got his name. Ah keep tellin' him tae chuck it but he widnae listen."

"Whit a sad story!" Annie said, "Where is he noo?"

Charlie shook his head.

"Wee Wrist? The last time Ah saw him was in a queue at the Royal Infirmary."

"Ye were askin' whit kinda dug Rin-Tin-Tin was?" Ina said.

Charlie nodded.

"It was a alsatian," Ina said.

"Ah!" Charlie exclaimed, "A German Shepherd!"

"Ah-Ha!" Wullie said, slapping his thigh.

"Ah knew it, Ah jist knew it. Your faither was brainwashed by a dug.."

Annie shook her head at Wullie's outburst.

"Don't talk rubbish," she snapped.

Charlie saluted smartly and, once more, clicked his heels.

"Well," he said, "Ah'd better get on wi' ma rounds in case THEY come back. Wan o' the wardens telt me that that might've just been the first wave."

Steam blew out of Erchie's ears. How dare an air-raid warden remark on such a thing? HE, Special Constable Erchie McPherson, was the official authority in the Well Street region.

If anybody was to make any remarks it would be He and HE alone.

He tutted, "Not at all," he said pompously, "there wull be no more raids this night..or this Mornin' as it now is, Ah can assure youse of that. Youse can take ma word for it."

Suddenly the Air-raid sirens wailed and all eyes went to a red-faced Erchie.

"Aw, here we go again!" Annie groaned

"Ye'll need tae let the Luftwaffe intae yer confidence, Erchie," Wullie said with a wry smile.

Charlie Gallagher put his arm around Ina's waist and steered her towards the door.

"Ah'll protect ye Miss McLatchie," he whispered.

Ina fluttered her eye lashes.

"Ina," she said, "Ma name's Ina,"

Charlie gave her waist a squeeze and hurried out of the door and into the street. Neighbours were already in the street heading for the open pend where the shelter stood. Wullie who had grabbed the two wally dugs from the mantelpiece, had one eye on Charlie Gallagher and the other on the lookout for that obnoxious mouth organ player.

The cold red-bricked air raid shelter was almost packed as Wullie and company squeezed in. They were lucky to find space at the end of a bench near the entrance. Wullie gritted his teeth as the first, flat note came from a mouth organ at the other end of the shelter.

Chatter pervaded the entire little building. And laughter, too. For the thought of sudden oblivion never entered peoples' minds. The droning of the German bombers overhead was just an inconvenience. The devastation of Greenock and Clydebank could not and would not ever be forgotten. It only welled up in peoples' hearts a grim determination never to give in. But there's no doubt that deep down there was always that nagging fear that what happened in Greenock and Clydebank could easily happen here, in Well Street, in the Calton. But the terrible thought was pushed further and further into the recesses of the mind until it was ignored.

Wullie looked around the shelter. The sing-song had started

with, "There'll be Bluebirds Over the White Cliffs of Dover"...again. Wullie clapped his hands over his ears.

The mouth organ player ended the song on a perfectly flat note. But it was followed by loud applause and yelling for 'more'.

The wee man stood up and took his bow. "Would youse like for to perceive some Rimsky Corsokov?" he asked, showing off his classical talent.

Wullie stood up and cupping his hands around his mouth, megaphone fashion, yelled, "Ah'd rather perceive that you bugger off!" His words were re-echoed by a nun who was sitting near the mouth organ player. Sister Marie Teresa had studied music with the Vatican Samba Ensemble. Wullie noted that Charlie Gallagher's hand had slipped into Ina's sitting nearby. Erchie McPherson, who, after ushering them all into the shelter, had returned to the street to take command of things. Halfway through 'Mairzy Doats and Dozy Doats' he dashed in, holding up his arms, shouted out, "Keep calm everybody. Everything is under control...it's only bombs!"

"Thank God for that!" Wullie replied. "For a while there Ah thought they were peltin' us wi' snawba's. It's cauld enough in here."

Erchie scowled at Wullie before vanishing outside again where his authority would be recognised.

Rita, who was sitting beside Wullie, stuck her arm through his and, chattering, said, "Oh, Ah hope this raid disnae last long. Ah must try an' get a wee sleep before Ah go on duty this mornin' Ah'm on the number nine route, Auchenshuggle tae Dalmuir West. That's always a busy route. An, no' only that, Ah was hopin' tae get tae Barraland tonight again..."

"Again?" Wullie said, raising his eyebrows.

"Oh aye," Rita enthused, "Bully McGregor's got a new singer. Ye should hear him singin' 'Yours'" Rita sighed. "It reminds me o' Raspy. It's wan o' his favourites."

"Aye, well it's a bit mair romantic than 'Ye Canny Shove yer Granny Aff a Bus, that's for sure," Wullie said.

The Ack-Ack guns, based at nearby Glasgow Green, could be heard thundering and spitting their fire into the dark sky. Explosions could be heard as the German bombs found their targets. But mostly in the distance. At each crashing explosion Rita's nails dug into Wullie's arm.

The mouth organ player had decided to take a rest and Wullie was grateful. He found the sound if the anti-aircraft guns more tuneful and wished he had gone down to the Glasgow Green shelters where they had an accordion player who once played for the Empire's pit orchestra.

It was rumoured that Sir Harry Lauder, the internationally known Scottish comedian-cum-singer might pay a visit to the shelters. He had already appeared at John Brown's Shipyards, in Clydebank and gave an impromptu concert to the grateful workers. Wullie hoped that he would pay a visit to the shelters, particularly this shelter, up the 'pen', in Well Street. He reckoned he would be better than the current musical entertainment.

Wullie closed his eyes and listened to the distant explosions. He wondered what poor unfortunates were on the receiving end. At times the sounds came from 'way down Gallowgate' and, at other times, from the east, towards Bridgeton. He cursed the fact that he could do nothing. He was sitting here in this damned, damp air-raid shelter feeling completely useless!

In May 1940, not long after the war began, Foreign Secretary Anthony Eden called for men up to the age of sixty-five to join Anti-Paras units to guard installations such as factories and power stations against attack from German parachutists. They would be called the L.D.V. - Local Defence Volunteers, later to be changed to The Home Guard.

But a sniper's bullet from the first war, that chipped a foot bone, was enough for Wullie to be rejected. At the time he blessed that sniper as it was enough to get him repatriated from the mud, blood and gore of the bloody battlefields of France. Now he cursed him for not allowing him to do his bit. If only he could get into it, he thought, he'd show them. But he couldn't fault the young men of today who were in there fighting tooth and nail for HIS freedom. It was with admiration he stood at George Square and watched the 2nd Battalion Cameronians march past Lord Provost Paddy Dolan, who took the salute. They were resplendent, the brass buttons gleaming, kilts swishing and bayonets glistening, catching the morning sunlight. He would see these young fighting men again , he was sure, at that same spot...only during a Victory Parade.

A Bomb blast nearby shook the shelter and dust showered down from the roof. Some of the women screamed and toddlers began to cry. Wullie jumped to his feet as Erchie McPherson hurried in.

"Don't panic!" he called, "it landed at the top of street, on the playground... an open space."

A sigh of relief swept round the shelter.

Annie, too, was watching Charlie and Ina. If Ina had, at last found love then Annie was happy for her. But she wished that it was Wullie sitting here holding hands with their next door neighbour. Rita noticed her mother gazing at the lovers.

"They're a picture, uren't they?" she commented.

Annie sighed, "It reminds me o' the time Ah used tae staun' up the close wi' yer da'.... haudin' his haun's." She sighed again.

"You held ma da's haun's when youse winched up the close?" Rita cried. She could not picture Annie and Sammy EVER standing winching.

"Oh, aye," Annie said. "Ah HAD tae haud his haun's, hen.Ah think that's the reason he's so good at semaphore."

"Ma Rasputin has never wance did anything oot o' place," Rita said.

"Ye worry aboot him, hen, don't ye?" Annie said softly

Rita nodded, "Ah know Ah shouldnae," she said, "Ah mean, he IS a genius. He telt me in his last letter that he has invented a gun that shoots roon' coarners." There was pride in Rita's voice.

"My, that's wonderful!" Annie cried. "How does it work?"

"Well," Rita began, "the wey Ah read it is that ye press yersel' against the wa' o' the buildin' and slowly move alang till ye come tae the end o' the buildin' then ye quickly stey where ye are, pressed against the wa', extend yer erms wi' the gun in yer haun's, point it roon' the coarner and fire."

Annie was very proud of her son-in-law.

"He's a genius, so he is!" she said.

"He's a chancer!" Wullie said.

Rita turned on him. She would never allow anybody say anything detrimental about her Rasputin.

"Listen, Uncle Wullie", she snapped, "you have nae idea of the geniusestic skills ma Rasputin's got. When he was younger he was known as 'The Miracle Worker'. When he was born his maw took him tae a clairvoyant."

"Ah heard she had tried tae gie him away," Wullie said.

"She wisnae tryin' for tae gie him away," Rita replied, her voice raised. "His maw knew there was somethin' different aboot him the minute she saw him efter he was born."

"He had three legs?" Wullie said snidely.

"NAW, NAW" Rita said, "she knew there was somethin' there...he OOZED somethin'"

"A' weans ooze somethin' an' we a' know whit that is."

"The calirevoyant said he had an aura aboot him," Rita said.

"Aurat crap!" Wullie said turning up his nose. "He was a miracle worker, ye were sayin, eh?"

"Aye, he was, " Rita replied. "In fact a loat o' people called him, Lourdes."

"Lourdes Plunkett, eh?" Wullie said.

"It happened when he gave an auld man the power tae speak clearly," Rita said proudly."

Wullie was impressed.

"He gave the auld man his voice back?" he said.

"He gave him his teeth back," Rita said. Their eyes met and they burst out laughing.

Annie joined in, "Aye," she said, "Always puttin' a smile on yer face, that man," she said.

Erchie McPherson decided to return to the street. He had been away too long and wondered how the wardens were managing to cope without his presence..

"Ah'll jist nip oot an' make sure everythin' goin' a'right," he said to Wullie.

Wullie nodded, "It's great to know ye're oot there, Erchie, lookin' efter us." Erchie failed to. catch the sarcasm in Wullie's voice. "Keep yer eyes open in case Auld Jake's McLatchie's oot there flashin' in the blackout" Wullie added.

Ina overheard Wullie's facetious remarks and turned on him, "Ma faither never flashed in his life!" she stormed.

"He never FLUSHED either," Wullie said, "See goin' intae that lavvy oan the stair landin' efter he came oot..." he grimaced, "It was like wadin' through a rain forest in the wake o' a herd o' diarrhoeaic elephants."

"That's no' nice, Wullie," Annie rebuked.

"Oh, you've experienced it an a'?" he said.

Annie drew him a 'look' and turned away.

Erchie was all ears. "Auld Jake's deid, remember?" he said.

"His traitorous ghost is goin' aboot, Erchie," Wullie said seriously. "An' don't forget him and Hitler are lie that," Wullie crossed his fingers. "Their cats get oan well, as well," he added."Besides," he said, "Ah am nut talkin' aboot fly flashin'. Ah am talkin' aboot TORCH flashin'... signallin' tae his Luftwaffe pals up there."

"Don't be daft!" Annie scowled. "Even if he WIS oot there flashin', whit could be tell them anywey?"

"He could tell them that Ah'm angry," Wullie said, puffing his chest out.

"Oh, Ah see," Annie said, "So they'll immediately report back tae Goring, Throw the towel in, mein herr, Wullie McSorley's angry."

"Mock if ye like," Wullie said sulkily.

"Well Ah can see that ye might well be angry," Annie said.

Wullie knitted his brows, "Whit dae ye mean?" he asked.

"Look!" Annie said.

Charlie and Ina were dancing cheek to cheek. And, what pleased Annie was, that Ina would now steer Charlie's feet towards Wullie and, provokingly sway in time to the music.

Wullie showed no interest in Ina's sexual flaunting. Turning to Annie, he snapped, "Whit dae ye mean Ah'll be angry?"

"The very fact that ye're bitin' the nose aff me proves it," Annie said.

"It jist means ye're stickin' yer nose in where it's no' wanted," Wullie said.

"Aye, well, we'll see," Annie said "ye're gonny lose her, y'know."

"Ah'm worried sick, int Ah?" Wullie snapped.

"Aye, ye ur!" Annie said, "Ah can see the green-eyed monster lurkin' in yer eye," she said.

"Ye're haverin'!" Wullie said.

"Am Ah?" Annie said with a slight smile.

"Ah telt ye," Wullie went on, "MA ideal wumman is Mae West. There's naebody can touch her!" he gave a click of the tongue.

"Wullie, staun two yerds away frae her and ye can touch her," Annie said sarcastically.

Both turned quickly on hearing a cry of delight from Rita.

Rasputin, in the full uniform of the Pioneer Corp, was standing at the shelter entrance. Rita ran and threw herself into his arms.

"Oh, Raspy, ye're hame!" she whooped.

Rasputin Plunkett squeezed her tightly. "Aye, Ah went up the stair but noticin' the hoose was empty."

"Ye knew it wis empty, Rasp?" Wullie said snidely.

Rasputin nodded, "Aye, when Ah saw the hoose was empty Ah guessed youse were a' doon here in the air-raid shelter because there was an air raid goin' on."

Annie kissed him on the cheek. "Welcome hame, son," she said.

Wullie, too, greeted him with a hearty handshake.

"But Ah thought ye were goin' on a special mission tae France," Rita said, squeezing his arm.

Rasputin looked at her quizzically, "How did you know Ah was goin' tae France?" he said, "that was top secret."

"Ye gave us a clue when ye spelt Frank wi' a 'C'?" Rita said.

Rasputin vigorously shook his head. "Naw, naw, ye've got it wrang," he said.

"It was China, wint it?" Wullie said with a smug expression.

"Naw it wisnae," Rasputin said, wondering how Wullie could have thought that.

"Well, why did ye miss oot the 'K' and put in a 'C', gein' a' us the wrang impression?" Wullie said.

"'Cos Ah'm a rotten speller," Rasputin said with some shame.

Wullie shook his head in disbelief. "So, where DID ye go oan this dangerous mission...Blackpool?" he said mockingly.

Rasputin stroked his chin as he re-lived the dangerous mission from which he had just returned.

"Naw," he said, his chin thrusting out, "it WAS France right enough. Ma assignment was tae capture a top German general. Ah had orders for tae bring him back tae Blighty. That posed a terrible problem!"

"How come?" Wullie asked, suddenly interested.

"Ah didnae know whare Blighty was," Rasputin said. "And when Ah asked them they jist laughed."

"An' whit happened, son?" Annie said, proud that her daughter's 'man' had been given such an important mission.

Rasputin continued to stroke his chin — a faraway look in his eyes. "Well," he said, "this was a General Von Runstadt, Ah had tae capture. Ah was parachuted doon and Ah stealthily made ma wey tae the bivouac he was steyin' in."

Wullie's brows shot up, "A General.. steyin' in a TENT?" he cried in disbelief.

"Aye," Rasputin said, "a' the chateaux were filled."

Wullie, now hooked, drew nearer. "So, whit happened?" he said, excitement in his voice.

"Well, Ah sneaked up an' crawled intae the tent. He was lyin' sleepin' in bed an' Ah immediately threw the blannket ower his face. But he put up a terrible struggle an' Ah had tae clobber him ower the heid wi' a bed pan."

Wullie was wide-eyed, "He had a bed pan in the tent?" he asked incredulously.

"He had," Rasputin affirmed, adding quickly, "but it was empty. Anywey, Ah slung him ower ma shoulder and hurried away wi' him yellin' his heid aff. When we got tae oor rende-vouz point Ah put him doon and whipped the blanket aff him an' was shocked for to see that he had nae pyjamas on. He just stood there, naked as the day he was born an' callin' me for everythin'. But it didnae worry me. Ah just telt him, "You ur now a prisoner of war, General Von Runstadt. Well, he jist stood there...shiverin'."

"Whit did he say?" Wullie asked, finding new qualities in Rasputin.

"He said, 'Ah am nut General Von Runstadt, you bloody imbicile.' An' Ah telt him no' tae call me that or Ah'd chuck him oot the aeroplane when we took aff. 'Who ur ye, then?' Ah asked."

"An' whit did he say?" Wullie asked. "It wisnae Rommel, wis it?"

"Naw," Raspuitin said, shaking his head.

"Whit did he say his name wis?" Wullie asked, tightening his eyes.

"General Montgomery," Rasputin said shamefacedly.

Wullie laughed. "GENERAL MONTGOMERY? STAUNIN' THERE NUDE?"

Raputin nodded, "Aye," he said.

"The Full Monty, eh?" Wullie chuckled.

"Aye, he was ower there doin' a wee recce," Rasputin said. "They should've telt me, so they should. It was a' a big mix up."

The story reminded Wullie of his own daring days during World War One. His mind went back to the trenches where, after a fierce attack on the German lines, they had fallen back into their filthy, muddy trenches. How, in the blackness of night, he heard a faint voice coming across the battlefield. A weak voice crying for help. Wee Geordie Hamilton volunteered to crawl out and bring the victim in. But, being the corporal in charge, Wullie had stopped him. Besides, Wee Geordie had two wooden legs. He had tried to hide that fact but chronic woodworm had taken its toll and despite all his wily manoeuvres, Wullie saw through him. For when Wee Geordie joined the regiment he was six feet two and he was now four feet three and shrinking by the minute as the dreaded woodworm took its toll. He was soon known as 'The Walkin' Helmet'. And so Wullie crawled out that stinking, soaking wet night. On and on towards the distress call of that wounded comrade. But, alas, just like Rasputin, he was duped. The cry for help did not come from a wounded soldier at all. A German decoy parrot was waiting for him...as an unseen sniper was. The bullet grazed his foot just enough to have him repatriated. Wullie thanked that sniper for getting him away from that hellhole. The parrot, he took prisoner and , arriving back at the trench, ate it...giving a couple of legs to Wee Geordie.

And so he could say nothing derogatory about Rasputin's faux Par.

Annie was anxious to know about Sammy.

"Was ma Sammy wi' you when ye went tae France?" she asked Rasputin with a plea in her voice.

Rasputin was silent for a moment

"Aye, he was, " he said finally, adding, "We jumped frae the plane together....him first then me."

"And so he wis wi' ye when ye captured the general?"

"OOR ain General," Wullie rubbed in.

"Er...naw," Rasputin said hesitantly, "Ah saw him on the grun' when Ah landed right efter him but Ah decided for to go ahead masel' an' no' risk HIS life, Ah knew you would be worried and if anythin' happened tae him ye would blame me for insistin' he go wi' me. So Ah went masel'."

"Aw, that was awfu' thoughtful o' ye, Raspy'" Annie said, kissing his cheek.

"Besides," Rasputin went on, "his parachute didnae open."

ANNIE AND RITA WAILED TOGETHER.

"He landed heid first," Rasputing added.

"That's a'right then," Wullie said. "He wullnae have hurt hisel'!"

"Is... is he deid?" Annie said, having to stick her knuckle into her mouth.

"Naw, it was a soft bog we landed in. He was buried up tae his waist. His legs were stickin' up oot the grun' Ah had tae run when Ah heard the German patrol comin'."

"Oh, poor Sammy," Annie wailed, "he's that sensitive aboot his varicose veins. He'll no' even let me see them. And there he is showin' them aff tae the hale German army. His face would be purple, so it would."

"Seein' the position he was in, Ah'm inclined for to agree wi' ye, Annie," Wullie said.

"Am sure ma daddy wull be a'right," Rita said, "Nae prison camp can haud him. At least ma man's hame an' oot o' danger."

"Aye, well Ah've been trainin' for a new joab, hen." Rasputin said, "It'll be less dangerous than the Pioneer Coarps, cleanin' oot lavvies an' that. There wull be nae chance o' me catchin' germs."

"Aw, Ah'm gled, darlin'!" Rita said, squeezing his arm.

"Whit wull ye be daein' noo?"

"Ah'm gonny be a bomb disposal expert." Rasputin said, smiling.

"Aw, Raspy!!" Rita wailed.

"Don't worry, hen," Raspy said, giving her a comforting squeeze. "Maist o' the modern bombs Ah designed."

"Well, Ah hope they're mair successful than yer gun that shoots roon' coarners," Wullie said.

Annie kicked his ankle and scowled. Rasputin was not to be disheartened or Rita hurt. Rasputin ignored Wullie's remark. Turning to Rita, he took her hand in his and softly said, "Ah'll get mair money in ma new joab, hen. It'll gie us a chance for tae save up for a bungalow."

"Or even just a BUNG?" Wullie said.

Annie's mind was to full of Sammy's fate. She sobbed quietly and dabbed her eyes.

"Ma poor Sammy!" she whimpered.

Wullie nodded.

"Aye, he'll no' like bein' incarcarated, he said.

Annie howled louder, her hand coming up to her mouth, shocked at what Wullie had said. "Oh, they'll no' dae that tae him , wull they?" she cried, adding, "Sammy was always very proud o' his manhood."

"Incarcarated means imprisoned," Wullie quickly explained.

"O, thank God for that," Annie said with relief, "Ah thought ye meant they would cut aff..."

"Aye, Ah know whit ye thought," Wullie said quickly, adding. "He'll get used tae the Stalag."

"Oh Sammy isna fond o' hoarses," Annie said.

"Stalag has got nuthin' tae dae wi' hoarses," Wullie corrected.

Annie composed herself, "Aye, well, if he could escape wance, he can escape twice. He'll no' have that hale Pacific Ocean tae swim."

"Don't bet on it," Wullie said, "Ye know how Sammy gets loast. He's got nae sense o' direction."

"Whit makes ye think that?" Annie said, annoyed that anyone could say anything derogatory about her Sammy.

"Well," Wullie said, "whit aboot the time Ah had tae gie him directions how tae get tae the lavvy."

"That can happen tae anybody," Annie snapped.

"Oan yer ain stair landin'?" Wullie said.

Rita was listening intently to this conversation. "Was ma da' hurt badly?" she asked, turning to her husband.

Rasputin Plunkett shook his head, "Naw, hen," he said "As Ah made ma heroic an' darin' escape, Ah heard him bawlin' an' callin' they Jerries every name under the sun."

"That's ma da'!" Rita said with pride.

Rasputin and Rita joined Ina and Charlie on the dance 'floor'. The mouth organ played "If you were the only girl in the world" and they were still dancing when the 'All-Clear' siren screamed.

It was mid-morning now as they all spilled out of the shelter, crossed Well street and, yawning and stretching climbed the stairs at number twenty-seven.

Rita had missed some of her shift at the Ruby Street depot but this was not unusual at the depot because of the frequent air raids by the Luftwaffe. But the system never suffered and there was always a 'caur' clanging along with little waiting at the stop.

Sleep was catching up with Rita and she decided to have 'forty-winks' before reporting for duty. Rasputin, under protest, was ordered to take the couch while his young wife's slumber could go on undisturbed.

Annie, too, flopped into her bed and was soon sound asleep. But sleep had left Wullie. After replacing the wally dugs to their proper place on the mantelpiece above the range, he decided to go out for a 'Dauner'...a walk.

Putting on his heavy overcoat, he first went up to Mr Adams' newsagent's shop, in London Road, where he picked up his 'Bulletin' and a packet of three Woodbine and two Pasha cigarettes. He did not much like the Pasha but, to purchase the popular Woodbine, with its fine Virginia tobacco it was compulsory to accept the two Turkish cigarettes. Many smokers were convinced that the tobacco rolled in the cigarette paper had been replaced by camels dung.

Coming out of the shop, Wullie turned right and headed down London Road until he came to Glasgow Cross. He decided against turning up High Street and carried on along

Trongate, turning up Mitchell Street and on to George Square. The Square was one of the Luftwaffe's targets during their first night raid on the city, on September 18th,1940. But, as Wullie parked himself on bench, there was nothing to indicate it had ever happened.

He sat and watched the Glasgweigans hurrying about their business. He saw laughter and lovers, holding hands, oblivious to the hustle and bustle around them.

He watched the pigeons fly around, unconcerned by the war for people, despite the rationing, always found a morsel for the 'doos'.

The Square was alive with Khaki. He was impressed by the different style of the allied uniforms that crowded around. The squared hatted Polish soldiers, the Australian with their 'cowboy' hats with the brim turned up at the one side, the Canadians with their crown-pointed Boy Scout type hats and the Americans with their natty forage caps, the officers with peaked caps and two-toned uniforms, light trousers that complemented their well-tailored tunics.

There were the children tugging at GI sleeves and pleading: "Any gum, chum?" And more often than not they were handed a stick of chewing gum that sent them away chomping and happy.

Wullie took heart at the sight of all of these nationalities coming together to crush Hitler. He had met many Americans during his own fighting days and it did his heart good to see that they had come in again to join up with their British allies.

A van turning into the square made him turn. A crowd was already gathering around the van which suddenly produced a cinema screen and a film was shown proclaiming the virtues of National Savings. His eyes turned to the clip-clopping of two Clydesdale work Horses coming along George Street pulling a cart with a poster on its side saying "Save your waste food — and save your bacon! One ton of kitchen waste each week will provide food for forty pigs"

Nothing was to be wasted during this war. Iron railings around buildings and backcourts were dug up and sent to be melted down and turned into bayonets and other essential war materials.

Wullie pulled the collar of his coat up and opened up his newspaper. It was, naturally, full of the war news but other news managed to find space in the columns of The Bulletin. A wee boy had fallen off a dyke in Walkinshaw Street, in Bridgeton. Mr and Mrs Tommy McGrath's four sons, all serving in the Armed Forces were home to celebrate their parents' Silver Wedding Anniversary. Life was going on and German Intelligence would get the message. Wullie thought it was all very clever.

It was early afternoon now and the pigeons were getting their fill. Wullie rolled up his paper and stood up. Soon the starlings would invade the city skies in their squadrons dropping their messy cargo to splatter windows and clothes. And, later, perhaps more squadrons of another, nosier breed would groan over those same skies with a much more deadlier cargo.

Wullie crossed the crowded Square, crossed Ingram Street, dodging a White tram going to Milngave, and walked down Glassford Street. In Argyle Street he waited just a few minutes before catching a number twenty-six 'caur' going east, to Burnside. But he alighted in London Road, at Well Street and headed home.

Wee girls were taking advantage of the daylight and happily playing 'Peever', hopping and skipping with chalked 'beds' on the pavement. Boys were riding imaginary horses, skelping their hind quarters to spur them on. Wee Jessie McCormick was shouting up to her mother on the second floor of number twenty-nine for a Piece. The jammy sandwich, wrapped in newspaper was chucked over within seconds and Wee Jessie munched hungrily as joined her pals who were 'cawing' skipping ropes. She jumped in and skipped as the two girls who were 'cawing' the ropes chanted, "I call in ma sister, Jeannie..." and Wee Jessie would jump free of the ropes to allow Jeannie to take over, then she vacated the spot for Betty who jumped clear for Maisie and on and on it went.

Wullie smiled. The blackout would be on top of them soon enough. But the 'weans' had enjoyed themselves while they could and had thumbed those snotty noses at the clouds above.

THREE

LE MAISON DE MADAME PETITE NELLIE WAS QUIET WHEN INA McLatchie entered. Nellie, a small lady with dyed-blonde hair and crimson finger nails, and who described herself as Coiffeuse to the Elite, was busy varnishing those long, glossy nails. She rose immediately Ina entered and approached her, extending the hand she had still not got around to.

"Ah! Madame Bawface!" she exclaimed.

Ina furrowed her brows at the greeting. "Hello, Madame Wee Nellie!" Ina said, ignoring the rude remark.

"Madame's face is more Baw than usual" Nellie went on, steering Ina to the chair. "Has Madame been eating balloons?"

Ina laughed, not taking the banter seriously. "Oh," she said, "you're a wee wag, Madame Wee Nellie," she said.

Madame Wee Nellie puckered her brows. "No, I haff never been in zat country," she said.

"Whit country?" Ina asked, puzzled. "Ah just said ye were a wee wag."

"Aw" Nellie said, throwing up her arms and chortling loudly, " I thought vous said a wee wog."

Madame Wee Nellie stood behind the chair and fluffed up Ina's hair.

"It's been a wee while since Ah've been in for to see ye," Ina said, almost apologetically.

"It's been ze BIG while!" Nellie exclaimed. "Haff vous been cutting vous own hair with a knife and fork?"

"Oh, Ah know it's a mess. But you wull soon have me looking good, Madame Wee Nellie."

"Oh, tut-tut," Nellie said, "Vous is a very old customer who comes here every five years or so. So, please, do not be so formal. Zis Madame Wee Nellie is for ze new customers. Vous can call me Madame Wee."

47

"Oh, thank you, Madame Wee" Ina said.

"Ze last time vous was here, if I remember," Nellie went on, "was to catch ze eye of somebody called Vullie, non?"

Ina nodded, "Aye, Wullie McSorley. Ah thought Ah'd got him wan night in the air-raid shelter. He was enamoured wi' ma soday scoanes."

"Well, I think vous has a soday heid," Nellie said." If vous canny get zem during an air-raid, vous wull never get zem!"

"Ah jist don't know whit tae dae!" Ina said sadly.

Nellie shrugged, "I don't know vhy vous vorry," she said, "I saw zis Vullie von day and he remined me of zat bottile off perfume over zer."

Nellie pointed to an array of bottles on a counter.

Ina smiled, "He oozes an aroma?" she said.

"Non, he iss a vee squirt," Nellie said. "So, vous is still chasing him, non?"

Ina blushed, "There is another man who has made it known that he fancies me," she said shyly. "A man in uniform!"

Nellie threw up her hands, "Voila!" she exclaimed, "I luff z mans in uniforms. He iss a Royal Navy capatain, non? Maybe a fighter pilot, eh?"

Ina shook her head, "Naw, he's oor milkman," she said quietly.

"So, vot ze hell, he's a man!" Nellie cried. "If ze Germans vin zis var zer vill be plenty off mens going about.

Ina was shocked, "Oh, Madame Wee Nellie!"

"Madame Vee, plees," Nellie interrupted.

"Aye, ye... ye... widnae fraternise wi' the German sojers, would ye?" she said with concern.

Nellie screwed up her nose, "Non, non, I vould neffer fraternise vith ze sojers who occupy my country. But I vould probably haff to change ze name off my salon, non? I vould not like zem speaking ze French language. I vould feel like ze collaborator.

Ina nodded, "Aye, Ah know whit ye mean," she said, "Whit would ye call yer salon? Le Maison Du Madame Petite Nellie is such a lovely name. It... it's so...so...French."

"How aboot 'Mein Herr'?" Nellie said and they both burst out laughing.

"Naw, but really, Madame Wee," Ina said, breaking off, "Would ye no' shut up yer shoap rather than gie THEM yer expertise?"

"No, no," Nellie cried, "Vhy should I go out of ze business, eh?"

That was not the answer Ina expected from this true French patriot. "Ye mean, if a German sojer came in, ye'd cut his hair?" she said incredulously.

"I vould cut his throat," Nellie said and, once more, they guffawed.

"Oh, ye are wan!" Ina said, giggling.

"Non, non, Ah'm no', don't let the deep voice fool ye, hen. Ah've got a bad cauld!"

"Ah!" Ina exclaimed, "yer accent has slipped...again!"

Nellie shook her head despairingly

"Ye know," she said, "there are days when Ah can keep it up and there are other days."

"Jist like me," Ina said, "Ah sometimes slip intae Gaelic and naebody knows whit Ah'm talkin' aboot. It worries me sometimes!"

"How's that?" Nellie asked.

"Ah don't know any Gaelic," Ina said, "No' only dae folk no' know whit Ah'm talkin' aboot... Ah don't know whit Ah'm talkin' aboot."

"Aye," Nellie admitted, "ma only connection wi' La Belle France is that Ah live in French Street up Dalmarock Road an' Ah like Maurice Chevalier."

"Well", Ina said, "as long as yer customers are happy! Ah'll no' tell anybody."

"Ye've got tae dae these things," Nellie said, "it's good for business. But Ah'm Glesca through and through," she said with pride in her voice, adding, "Ah've got that wee bit toughness aboot me!"

"Ah don't think there's anythin' tough aboot ye," Ina said. "In fact Ah think ye're rather delicate."

Nellie shook her head. "Naw, naw," she said, "Ah KNOW Ah've got that wee bit toughness in me. Ye hiv tae hiv if ye're gonny run yer ain business. It's the wey Ah was brought up. Ma da' was a hard man. When he took me doon tae the chapel for tae get baptised, he made sure the priest used dirty watter."

"An' ye think that's whit made ye tough?" Ina asked.

Nellie nodded, "Withoot a doot!" she said. "In oor street ye had tae be tough. When we played Kick-the-Can, we laid the can doon oan the grun' and kicked each other."

"That IS tough!" Ina exclaimed.

"Aye, naebody wore 'sonnies' in oor street. Hauf the weans used crutches."

"Ah can imagine!" Ina said.

"There wurnae many smiles in oor street, Ah can tell ye," Nellie continued, reminiscing. "Few o' the weans had teeth. But, it was the makin o' ye. We a' grew up eatin' mince."

The two woman were silent, Nellie to her childhood thoughts and Ina to the scheme she was about to launch. Nellie finally broke the silence. Fluffing up Ina's hair, she said, "Right! Let's see whit we can dae for vous!"

They laughed together. Nellie came round to the front of the chair and, cupping her hands under Ina's chin, she surveyed her face.

"Y'know," she said, "lookin' at your coupon, ye're lucky tae get a milkman!"

Ina shifted uneasily on the chair. She did not want to fight with Nellie as the petite hairdresser was the best around.

"Some men find me attractive," Nellie said.

"But dae ye get on wi' their dugs?" Nellie asked.

"Whit dugs?" Ina asked, raising her eyebrows.

"Their guide dugs," Nellie said, with a cheeky smile.

"That's no' very nice," Ina said.

"Is that whit ye say when ye look in the mirror?" Nellie said, keeping up the banter.

"Noo, let's see whit we can dae for you... whit miracle Ah can perform."

She walked over to her work top and returned with an implement.

Noticing Ina curiously watching her, she held it up, "Tongs," she said –

"Ya Bass," Ina said, completing the well known Glasgow phrase.

"Ye know somethin'?" Nellie said, "Ah'll never have for tae chinge the name o' this shoap 'cos the jerries wull never win this war."

"Ye're so sure?" Ina said, raising her brows.

"How could they," Nellie said, "when we've got the two Johns on oor side?"

"The two Johns?" Ina asked questioningly

"Aye, John Mills an' John Wayne," Nellie laughed. "Noo, let's hiv a look at yer cranium."

Nellie surveyed Ina's bonce from every angle.

"Tae tell ye the truth, Madame Wee," Ina said, "Ah want ye tae somethin' very special for me."

"Ah've got nae Polyfilla in the shoap," Nellie said without smiling.

"Naw, listen...." Ina pulled Nellie's head down and whispered in her ear.

Nellie burst out laughing.

"Really?" she chuckled.

"Aye, really," Ina said with satisfaction. "Oh, aye...WONDERFUL, hen, jist WONDERFUL."

Both laughed loudly as Nellie began to work.

Annie had slept through most of the afternoon and Rita had gone to work after a short rest. Rasputin had retired to the bed now and was glad to get off the couch. He would accompany Rita later, in the evening, to Barrowland and enjoy what was left of his short leave. Annie poured out two glasses of V.P. wine and offered one to Wullie, who was tuning in the wireless but not finding a station to his liking. He switched it off in disgust.

"Here," Annie said, " have a wee drink."

Wullie smacked his lips and took swig. "Ye canny beat the real McCoy," he said, wiping the back of his hand across his mouth.

"Ah was gled o' that wee sleep," Annie said, "although Ah could've slept on. They bloomin' air raids get ye doon, so they dae."

"Don't let them, Annie," Wullie said. "Don't let them demortalise ye, that's whit they're countin' on...demortalisin' everybody."

His Malapropism went over Annie's head.

"An' Ah'm worried aboot ma Sammy," she said, flopping on to the chair at the table.

"It should be his guards ye should be sorry for," Wullie said with a twinkle in his eye. "If he starts singin' nut only wull they turn a blind eye if he should try tae escape. They wull gie him the keys o' his cell and a railway ticket."

"Och, Wullie," Annie rebuked, "Sammy's no' as bad a singer as a' that!"

"Ur ye kiddin?" Wullie cried. "Whit aboot that night he was haufstoned an' started tae sing 'Nellie Dean'? He'd jist started when the hale buildin' emptied wi' everybody runnin' doon tae the air-raid shelter. They a' thought it was the sirens."

"Och, you exaggerate," Annie sniped. "But Ah canny help worryin' aboot him. Ah miss him an' a' the good times we had together...nights oot at the Geggie, the Wee Royal, the Queens pantomimes...wi' Ivy Val an' Sammy Murray an' Frank an' Doris Droy. Jack an' May Short, at the Metropole. Efter the shows we'd go intae the Chrystal Bell pub , opposite the Queens, in Watson Street, at Glesca Croass and Ah'd have a wee port and Sammy would have a big Johnny Walker. Then we'd get a fish supper for me an' a black puddin' supper for him oot o' Ina's chip shoap, in Stevenston Street. Happy days, Wullie. Noo we've got this terrible war wi' the boys goin' away tae fight. A loat o' them hardly oot o' school. An' a loat o' them wullnae have that happiness Sammy an' me have known 'cos they'll no' come back.

Where's it a' gonny end?"

Annie sighed. She felt lighter as though she had just relieved herself of a heavy burden. Wullie took the bottle and poured two large drinks.

"Here, hen," he said, holding one out for Annie. "This is a' a bad dream and it WULL come tae an end wan day. And ye'll be able tae dae a' they things again wi' Sammy."

Annie sipped and, looking over the rim of her glass, said, "D'ye...ye.. really think his parachute didnae open?"

Wullie laughed, "Don't be daft," he chuckled, "Rasputin was havin' ye on. Ye know how he thinks he's a Tommy Morgan. He was just makin' light o' the hale thing so ye widnae worry."

52

"WIDNAE WORRY?" Annie blurted. "Somebody tells ye yer man jumped oot o' an areoplane wi' a parachute that didnae work and landed oan his heid, buryin' hisel' right up tae his waist...his legs flayin' in the wind. WIDNAE WORRY?" Steam was jetting from Annie's ears.

"Ach, don't look at it that wey," Wullie said. "We know he's a' right and Ah'll bet ye he's hame before ye know it."

Annie, now quietened down, said, "Ah just hope ye're right, Wullie, Ah just PRAY ye're right."

They had two more refills and sat silently for a moment.

"Whit dae ye think o' Ina?" Annie said at last.

"No' much," Wullie replied, taking a final swig.

"Naw, Ah mean aboot her faither manifestin' himsel'?"

"He used tae dae that oan the stair landin' hurryin' doon tae the lavvy," Wullie said.

"She must've got the fright o' her life!" Annie exclaimed.

"No' as big a fright as HE got seein' her in her tied up curlers, Ah'll bet," Wullie said.

"That's no' a nice thing tae say, Wullie," Annie said disapprovingly.

"And another thing, Wullie went on, "Ah do nut believe her faither was an actor that went tae Hollywood or was ever in a picture wi' Rin-Tin-Tin, the great dug actor."

"Oh aye, he was," Annie said adamantly, "Ah saw that great picture when Auld Jake an' Rin-Tin-Tin, that great dug actor, were on a boat. Wan minute they were sittin' there sittin' hivin' a drink in the lounge o' the Titanic an' the next minute they were in a rowin' boat, rowin' for their lives as the big liner sank beneath the waves. It was that touchin', so it was. They were freezing and, for three days an' nights, they had tae huddle together an' hug each other for tae keep waarm. Then they were picked up. Poor Jake had tae take tae his bed efter that scene an' they had tae get the doactor."

"Pheumonia?" Wullie asked.

"Distemper," Annie replied.

"Ah still don't believe it, "Wullie said, "Wi' Auld Jake gone, Ah have inherited a lavvy. Did you know he used tae take his wind-up gramophone doon tae the cludgie wi' 'im? "

"Music while he worked?" Annie said mischievously,

adding, "He loved music, so he did!"

"Have ye ever stood oan that landin' freezin' an'waitin' tae get in tae that lavvy....an' hivin' tae wait 'cos that auld swine was hivin' a concert in there?"

"Poor auld sowel!" Annie said.

"Poor nuthin'," Wullie snapped. "Ah mean, Ah widnae have minded a quick chorus of Red Pails in the Sublets but tae staun' there crossed legged, through the hale o' Madame Butterfly. Ah ask ye!"

"Aye, he DID like his opera," Annie said.

"Aye, but when it ended the lavvy door would fly open and there he was staunin' erect, salutin' as they played ' God Save the King'. Nut a pretty sight, Annie!"

"He was very patriotic, tae!" Annie said in the old man's defence.

"Ah danced wi' joy when Ah thought we'd got rid o' him," Wullie said with a dismal expression. "But noo...?"

"Ah wonder if Ina really saw him?" Annie said, knitting her brows.

"It's hard tae imagine," Wullie said.

"Well, Ah'll tell ye somethin' for nothin'," Annie said sharply. "That milkman, Charlie, is oot tae get her...and he will!"

Wullie shrugged, "He's welcome!" he said.

"You don't mean that and you know it," Annie said angrily. "You've got a soft spot for her, Ah know."

"Ye mean ye found the title deeds in ma drawer?" Wullie sniped.

"Don't be so sarcastic!" Annie said sternly. "Ye know fine well that ye like Ina McLatchie mair than ye care tae admit."

"Whit makes ye think that?" Wullie said, avoiding Annie's gaze.

"Ah sometimes catch ye lookin' at her," Annie said.

"Ye canny help lookin' at her, can ye? No' wi' a coupon like that," Wullie said, still looking away.

"Noo, that's no' true," Annie said. "Ina is a fine lookin' girl", she said with some affection in her voice.

"That's a lie for a start," Wullie retorted. "GIRL? She must be at least eighty-four,"

"Ina is probably a bit younger than me." Annie said. "And Ah know she likes you a lot. But ye're gonny lose her and ye've only yersl' tae blame."

Wullie did not reply. They sat in silence and it was Annie who, once again broke the quietness. She had been thinking of Rita, losing her sleep for most of the night because of the air raid. Of Rasputin coming home and of how Rita had to force herself out to the Ruby Street Tram Depot as though nothing had happened.

She turned to Wullie, "Poor Rita," she said, "had tae go tae her work efter bein' up hauf the night an' her man just arriving' hame for a wee leave."

Wullie, being his usual facetious self, nodded, "Aye, right enough. Just as long as Jerry disnae know he's at hame. They might take advantage o' his absence and invade us."

Annie did not appreciate Wullie's sarcasm. "Noo listen Wullie," she said angrily, "Rasputin is a fine boy who's daein' his bit. Ye shouldnae put him doon."

Before Wullie could say anything there was a loud knock on the door. Annie rose from the table.

"Ah'll get it!" she said and went out into the lobby. Wullie heard muffled voices and wondered what the chat was all about. He looked up as Annie entered...a smile on her face.

"It's somebody for you, Wullie," she said with that wry smile that worried Wullie. He rose from the table and his eyes trained expectantly on the door. And his jaw dropped as a buxom blonde sidled provocatively in.

"Geez! Mae West!" he drooled. But, taking a closer look, he saw the chubby features of Ina McLatchie.

Ina walked sexily towards him, her hips swaying and her arms outstretched. "Hello Big Boy," she purred. "Why don't you come up and see me sometime?"

"How? Are ye flittin' up tae the tap flat?" Wullie sneered.

Ina ignored the sarcasm and advanced stealthily, like a tiger going in for the kill.

"Ah's rollin' ma eyes at you, big boy," she said huskily.

"Aye, well Ah'll just roll them back," Wullie said.

But Ina was not going to be put off and continued to advance menacingly.

55

"Ye're lookin' stunnin', Ina," Annie complimented.

"It must be somethin' in the mulk!" Wullie growled, backing away from the determined Ina.

Grabbing two candlesticks from the mantelpiece he held them like a cross in front of him, Dracula fashion. "Get back! Back! Begone ya maniac," he snapped.

But Ina was not allowing herself to be rebuffed. Grabbing Wullie by the shoulders, she threw him across the table and threw herself on to him. Wullie groaned and then yelled to Annie for help.

"Annie, get this lump aff me," he screamed. But Annie stood, hands on hips and doubled up in laughter.

"But Wullie," Annie said, "ye said Mae West was yer ideal wumman."

"She is nut Mae West," Wullie said breathlessly.

"Ah've got everythin' Mae West's got," Ina protested, struggling to keep the writhing Wullie pinned to the table top.

"Aye, but yours is a' in the wrang places," Wullie gasped.

Nobody heard the door opening. Charlie Gallagher walked in unannounced and immediately took in the boisterous scene. Ina had managed to get her lips on to Wullie's tightly closed mouth who immediately wiped off the offending contact with the back of his hand and spat out ignominiously

Charlie's countenance took on its most aggressive expression. "Whit's this?" he demanded.

"They're just playin' a wee game o'... er...table tennis," Annie quickly said.

"It looks mair like blow fitba' tae me," Charlie said, puckering his lip.

"Naw, it's quite innocent," Annie replied.

But Charlie was not convinced. "Ah came up here," he said grudgingly, "for tae gie youse an extra pinta milk an' Ah find THIS! It's enough tae turn ma stomach."

"It's usually yer mulk that's turned," Annie said.

Charlie dashed across the room and pulled Ina and Wullie apart.

"Right you," he said in his most forceful tone, "Stoap this nonsense at wance. Efter a' YOU ur supposed tae be ma spouse tae be...an' that's a legitimate proposal."

56

"Ah am nut interested," Wullie said.

"HER, Ah'm talkin' tae HER," Charlie blurted and turning to a breathless Ina, went on, "Ina, ma darlin', wull you be mine?"

"Your whit?" Ina said.

Charlie took her hand in his and went down on bended knee. "Wull you be ma wife?" Charlie stood up. "You an' me together going through life hand in hand. Daein' the mulk round in the wee sma' 'oors...at six o'cloack...clippity-cloppin' roon a' the streets."

Ina pulled her hand away, "If you think Ah'm gettin' up for six o'cloack in the moarnin' an' puttin' oan ma high heels tae go oot wi' mulk, you are not on!" she snapped.

"YOU wull not be daein' the clippity-cloppin'," Charlie said. "That's Daisy, ma hoarse."

"Does yer hoarse wear high heels?" Wullie asked.

Charlie ignored the comment. "Say you wull be mine for to hold," he pleaded.

"Dae ye no' think Ina looks like Mae West, Charlie?" Annie said, embarrassed at the romanticism.

"Ah'd love her even if she looked like John West," Charlie drooled.

"Fishy, this!" Wullie commented. "You ur only efter her money, so ye are! The cash left tae her by her faither's faithful freen', Rin-Tin-Tin, the great dug actor — three million pounds and two-dozen cans o' Pal."

"Ah'd love her if she had only wan million," Charlie rasped.

"Ah-Ha!" Wullie said, slapping his thigh, "See! Ah was only testin ye. She has nae millions. A' she's got tae her name is tuppence ha'penny and four empty ginger boattles."

"Ignore him, Charlie," Ina said with a turn of heart. "For that's whit Ah'm gonny dae from noo on. He's had his chance. Ah gied him ma heart an' he's thrown it back at me.. three times. Whit ye might call a 'Triple By-Pass."

Charlie beamed, "Ye'll no be sorry, Ina," he slobbered. "You wull hiv everythin' yer heart desires – free mulk for life an' plenty o' manure for yer windae boax."

Charlie pulled her to himself and kissed her passionately.

Wullie found himself running a finger round inside his collar.

"Aye, Well Ah could believe that," he said, "You're full o' it."

Charlie threw him a contemptuous look. "Can Ah take it, then, that you have accepted ma proposal of marriage?" he said to Ina, squeezing her hand.

"Aye, ye can, Charlie," Ina replied, pecking him on the cheek.

"Aw, ma wee darlin'!" Charlie said, giving a jump of delight.

"Oh God!" Wullie groaned, "Ah'm gonny be sick!"

The lovers were not listening.

Gazing into Ina's eyes, Charlie said, "Ah'd have gied ye ma maw's weddin' ring, darlin', but Ah've got a sore back."

"Whit's yer back got tae dae wi' it?" Ina asked, raising her eyebrows.

"She's still wearin' it and she's buried in Sighthill," Charlie said apologetically.

"Ah do nut want you bringin' yer tons o' manure up them stairs," Wullie said angrily, "spillin' it a' ower the place. Wan dug up here is daein' enough damage."

Charlie dismissed Wullie's comment with a wave of the hand. Turning to Ina, he said, "You have made me the happiest man in the world, ma wee lamb," he sighed "We'll get married in St Alphonsus' an' have a honeymoon doon the watter, in Rothesay. An' we'll sit on the beach an' eat oor pokey hats."

"Ye canny sit oan the beach, "Wullie sniped.

"How no'?" Charlie said in a flat tone.

"'Cos you could be sittin' oan her faither who is reposing amongst the Rothesay pebbles," Wullie said smugly.

"Ah have heard a' aboot how you collected Ina's faither's ashes frae the undertaker and washed them doon a sink in the pub, possibly endin' up in Rothesay."

"Aye, well it was poetic justice," Wullie said. "Auld Jake loved goin' doon the watter but he never knew he'd be goin' there WI' the watter!"

Ina dabbed her eyes.

"Ah'll no' mind goin' tae Rothesay," she said between dabs, "Ah'll feel that wee bit nearer ma da'."

Wullie nodded, "If ye're sittin' oan tap o' him, Ah'd say ye couldnae get much nearer," he said. "Go tae Millport an' ye can sit anywhere ye like. Get intae the Ritz Cafe an' get a plate o' hoata da peas.. It'll take yer mind aff yer da'."

"We wull decide oorsl's where we wull go," Charlie sniped.

"Ah'm only tryin' tae help," Wullie said. "If ye really want a happy honeymoon, Ina, you go tae Rothesay an' HE can go tae Millport."

"You stoap inteferin'!" Charlie snapped.

Wullie shrugged as Charlie, taking Ina by the arm and steering her towards the door, cooed in her ear. "C'mon, darlin' and Ah'll introduce ye tae Daisy."

The couple left and Wullie and Annie sat in silence. Annie rose and began to tidy up, not because anything had to be tidied but just to keep active. She was sorry that Ina had given her heart to Charlie Gallagher. It had always been her wish that Ina and Wullie would tie the knot. For, despite Wullie's apparent disinterest, she was sure her brother DID, deep down, have a deep admiration for Ina McLatchie. At times she caught Wullie looking at Ina with a light in his eye. Wullie, of course, would deny it. But Annie was no fool and her woman's instinct told her that there's was some hope there. Now, it seemed, hope had gone.

Annie finally sat at the table with a sigh. "Well...?" she said looking over at Wullie, who was sitting staring blankly.

"Well whit?" he said.

"You've loast her!" Annie said flatly.

"So what?" Wullie shrugged.

"That lassie has deep affection for you," Annie said, trying to keep her anger under control. "You, and only God knows why, were the apple o' her eye." Annie gritted her teeth.

"Aye, well wan aipple disnae make a date," Wullie said.

Annie rose and stood menacingly over him.

"Ye've let happiness slip though yer fingers," she said, allowing her anger to show.

Wullie did not reply. He took up his newspaper and began to read, showing how unconcerned by it all. But Annie was not convinced.

A sudden anxious rapping at the door gave her a start. Erchie McPherson, not waiting for a reply, hurried breathlessly in shouting at the top of his voice...

"Annie...Wullie... hurry, hurry...get oot, QUICK!"

"Whit is it...whit is it?" Annie said, panicking.

"A BOMB!" Erchie gasped. "An unexploded bomb...up the pen'. It could go aff anytime. And if it goes aff WE go aff..."

"A BOMB?" Annie screamed in terror.

"A Bomb?" Wullie repeated, hurrying over to the mantelpiece and grabbing the two 'wally dugs' and hurrying towards the door yelling as loud as he could..."A BOMB!..EVERYBODY, A BOMB!"

Erchie kept calling them not to panic although his own heart was pumping furiously.

Wullie, followed by Annie and Erchie were blocked at the door as Rasputin, dressed in pyjamas and rubbing sleep from his eyes, stood there.

"Where's the lavvy key?" he asked. "Ah'm dyin' tae go!"

"Ah was dyin' tae go as well," Wullie volunteered, "but Ah don't need noo."

"The key's hingin' behind the ootside door," Annie yelled.

"Whit's a' the commotion?" Rasputin said.

"There's an unexploded bomb doon there and Ah, hivin' full authority regardin' action that should be taken if unexploded bombs should be discovered in ma province, order all of youse oot and doon tae the Glesca Green shelters."

"A BOMB! A BOMB!" Annie continued to panic, running into the bedroom and retrieving a biscuit tin containing her insurance policies from the top of the wardrobe.

Hurrying to the door, once more she was blocked by Rasputin who stood to attention with his hand up as though controlling traffic.

"Don't worry, Rasputin' here."

Annie's mind was in turmoil. Turning, she snapped at Wullie, "Get rid o' they dugs," she commanded.

"Ah am goin' naewhere withoot they dugs," Wullie said adamantly, "The were ma maw's dugs." He spoke reverently as though the wally dugs were relics.

Annie decided not to argue. There were more pressing problems at this particular moment.

Rasputin was taking the situation in his stride.

"Don't anybody worry," he said authoritatively. "Ah wull

attend tae this wee problem. This wull dae me well when Ah eventually join Bomb Disposal full time."

"You wull wait until the REAL Bomb Disposal squad gets here," Erchie commanded. "Ah am the senior officer in charge here!" Erchie stuck out his chest but it was pushed back in by Rasputin who snapped, "We have nae time tae hing aboot. Ah'll haun'le this. Ah am of the military."

At that point, Rita came hurrying in, still in her clippie's green uniform. "Whit's goin' oan, here?" she demanded.

"It's nothin' for tae worry aboot, hen," Rasputin said.

"Oh!" Rita said, "ye're up, Raspy. Had a wee sleep son? Ready for Barraland the night?"

"Look, "Wullie said impatiently, "if ye don't let him oot that door, we'll a' be goin' tae Barraland...ower the rooftaps."

Rita thought of Rasputin, wondering what dangers he faced and if she should ever see him again? She grabbed Rasputin's hand tightly. "Whit does he mean by that, Raspy?" she asked, a worried expression on her face.

"It's nothin', hen," Rasputin said, "Ah'm jist goin doon tae the pen's for tae tackle an unexploded bomb."

"A BOMB?" Rita exploded. "A BOMB? Aw, naw, Raspy...let somebody else dae it... you don't know anythin' aboot bombs."

"Rita, hen,"Rasputin said, "It jist might be wan Ah designed. Don't worry, hen, you'll see me comin' through that door before ye know it."

"No tae mention the windae, that wa' an' doon the lum," Wullie added.

Erchie was getting impatient. "C'mon youse," he said sternly.

Wullie sauntered over to the mantelpiece and replaced the 'wally dugs'. Ah'm goin naewhere," he said adamantly. "The Jerries have disrupted ma life enough and enough is enough!"

"Me, tae!" Rita said.

"And me," Annie concurred.

All three sat down at the table and folded their arms defiantly. Rita thrust a knuckle into her mouth and Annie put a comforting arm around her shoulder, knowing her daughter was worried about Rasputin.

Erchie turned at the door, "Ah canny be expected for to evict three of youse," he said, "but Ah had better get doon there and get alang tae the shelter."

Erchie strolled casually out of the house and then he would undoubtedly have won a gold medal at the Olympic Games as he took the stairs two at a time, rushed out of the close and streaked up Well Street, across London Road and down into Monteith Row and across the green, dodging the clothes poles and down into the first air-raid shelter he came to.

The shelter was packed with Well Street residents and many from Stevenston Street and Bain Street to the west and Claythorn Street to the east. The accordion player stopped in mid note as Erchie dashed, breathlessly in.

"It's a' right everybody," Erchie gasped. "Ah have come doon for to make sure youse are a'right. The bomb up the pen's is bein' attended tae by an expert. Noo, if Ah may, Ah would like to request a number frae oor talented accordion player, Cheerful Duggie Buggie...if youse don't mind?"

A chorus of "Nae bothers" and "On ye go, son", echoed round the shelter.

"Whit's yer pleasure, Constable?" Duggie Buggie asked, his fingers poised over the keyboard.

"Nearer My God to Thee," Erchie said, having to dodge the cushions pelting down on him.

The accordion player burst into "We'll meet again," and the spirits in the shelter rose and the cushion throwing stopped much to Erchie's relief as he joined in singing with gusto with the others.

Back at 27, Well Street, Rita wiped perspiration from her brow as Annie continued to comfort her. "He's a brave boy!" she said. "Don't worry hen."

Wullie nodded, "Aye, don't worry," he said, "if the bomb DOES go aff he'll no' feel a thing."

Rita wailed all the more and Annie glared at Wullie who turned away.

They sat in silence listening to the ticking of the mantelpiece clock. But, in their minds, that ticking was the same ticking Rasputin was hearing from the bomb.

"Oh, shut that cloack aff!" Rita cried, her nerves getting the better of her. Wullie obliged and sat down again in the silence.

The blast came quickly and unexpectedly. Rita cried out and jumped up. She buried her head in her mothers breast, "Oh Mammy?" she sobbed uncontrollably.

Annie patted her on the back and whispered softly, "There, there, hen...he was a true hero."

"Noo that he's deid in the line o' duty he'll get a medal," Wullie volunteered. And Rita wailed all the louder.

"WULLIE!" Annie yelled, reproving him.

Wullie shrugged and joined Annie at Rita's side. He kissed Rita lightly on her tear-stained cheek.

"Ah'm sorry, hen," he quietly said.

A sudden noise made them turn to the door. Rasputin, his pyjamas in tatters stood there with a grin on his face.

"Ah never got doon tae the bomb," he said, "Ah was dyin' tae go tae the lavvy an' Ah went there first."

Rita let out a whoop of joy and hurried over, throwing her arms around his neck with Wullie and Annie following on and slapping his back.

"Oh, Raspy!" Rita said, hugging him tightly.

"Ah was just sittin' there when Ah heard the explosion an' ma heid hit the roof. Ah wisnae sure if it was the bomb or that black puddin' supper Ah'd ate." he said.

They all laughed loudly. But it was a nervous laugh.

Annie immediately poured out four large glasses of V.P. wine and they toasted themselves.

All of them glad to be alive...at least until the next crisis.

Rita gave Rasputin a dig in the ribs. "Right," she said, "C'mon, you an' me are gettin' ready for Barraland."

"Aye," Annie said, "Life must go on. Ye're no' gonny let a wee thing like a bomb spoil yer fun, are ye?"

"Ye're right, Mammy, ye're dead right," Rita laughed and getting behind Rasputin, pushed him towards the door, said, "C'mon, ma boy, we've got a date wi' Billy McGregor and the Gaybirds."

FOUR

THE NIGHT WAS CRISP AND CLEAR AS RASPUTIN AND RITA STEPPED out of the closemouth into Well Street. A bright, full moon bathed the black asphalt in a glistening glow

The brightness of the night was, in one way, welcome. It allowed pedestrians to dodge the baffle walls that stood outside every closemouth — a hazard which had caused as many injuries as the bombings. Also it was possible to see traffic. For often the yellow slits of cars headlights were on top of you before you knew it and there were many serious injuries and even fatalities caused by road accidents. Trams, or the 'caurs' as they were affectionately called had blacked out windows but a stroller could hear them coming. Drivers were not sparing with their warning bells. At the same time this bright night was the Luftwaffe's bonus. This was a 'bomber's moon' and on such nights the air-raid wardens and the ack-ack squads were on double alert. The A.F.S., the Auxiliary Fire Service was fully manned and at the ready. Wardens were stationed on high buildings on the look-out for the squadrons of Heinkel Bombers, the Local Defence Volunteers' rifles were well lubricated and ready for action. The Glasgow Corporation Rescue Service trucks were fully manned with full tanks, ready to dash to any scene where they were urgently required. The Y.W.C.A and the W.V.S., The Women's Voluntary Service, were ready with their mobile canteens. Firewatchers were on the alert and wardens and special constables paraded the streets, ever watchful for the slightest chink of light coming from a careless window. The city was alert but life went on and Rasputin and Rita had none of this tenseness on their mind as they headed up Well Street, across the children's playground and on to Gallowgate, with its clanging, blacked out 'caurs'. They were sorry that the 'Mussel's shop' was closed and the treat of a bag of 'wulks' or a plate of steaming mussels was denied them. They were pleased to see that only a few were left in the queue for Barrowland. Most of the queue was made up of G.I.'s, American servicemen billeted at the yellow bricked, imposing Beresford Hotel, in Sauchiehall Street, and although leaving the hotel's entrance, the soldiers, turning right towards Charing Cross would pass the Astoria dance hall and the glitzy, luxurious Locarno, where many made for, others headed down east to Gallowgaete and the Barrowland Ballroom which not only had the great Billy McGregor Band but also had a 'Jitterbugging Corner' — American jiving which was frowned upon by more conservative dance halls. The G.I.'S also had the Albert Ballroom near their billets. Many preferred to stay near their hotel and many others headed for the Plaza, on the south side or along to the Dennistoun Palais where Laurie Blandford and his Broadcasting Band played.

Green's Playhouse, in Renfield Street was just a ten-minute walk away , along Sauchiehall Street and a popular venue for the Britain's star bands - Ted Heath, Joe Loss, Ken McIntosh and many others. Many a romance blossomed under its twinkling chandelier and got on track to the tune of 'Take the A Train'.

Rita made straight for the 'Ladies Room' as they entered the ballroom. And, after preening herself, she emerged to join Rasputin at the side of the dance floor. The band were swinging with Glenn Miller's 'In The Mood' and the jivers were whooping it up in the 'Jitterbugging Corner'. Rasputin nodded towards the jivers and said, "Fancy?"

Rita nodded and the pair joined in. Most of the other dancers were Americans who made the dance their very own. As the last note faded, Rasputin and Rita ambled over to the side, a little breathless but exhilarated.

"That was brilliant!" Rasputin said.

"Phew! In the Mood!" Rita gasped.

"No' the noo, hen," Rasputin said, "no' in front o' a' these people."

"Ah'm just sayin' that was the name o' that song," Rita said.

"Oh!" Rasputin said, surprised, "Ah thought it was Campbelltown Loch Ah wish you were Whisky."

"Whit made ye think that?" Rita asked drawing her eyebrows together.

"'Cos Ah'm always thinkin' o' whisky," Rasputin said.

Rita took a step back, surprised. "Aw, Raspy," she cried, "don't tell me ye've started drinkin'?"

Rasputin' took on the air of a naughty boy who had been caught out on some misdemeanour. He looked down, making a pattern on the floor with his pointed toe.

"Ach, ye know how it is, hen," he said apologetically. "We're a' in there ...a' buddies taegether...trained killers every wan and a' livin under the wan roof in that big tin hut...forty o' us.. We're like a coiled spring just waiting tae go intae action. Just waitin' tae get ower there and finish the job. Ye cany help but want a wee drink. It's a' part o' the gemme!"

"Just as long as ye don't drink too much," Rita said. "Whit's yer pleasure?"

"Ah telt ye tae wait till we get hame. Ye're awfu' anxious, Rita!"

Rita could not believe what she was hearing. Her jaw dropping open and blurted out, "Whit ur you talkin' aboot? Ah'm askin' whit it is ye drink, that's a'."

"Aw!" Rasputin grinned, "Ah thought ye meant..."

"Ah know whit you thought," Rita said, hiding a smile.

"Well," Rasputin went on, "as faur as the drink goes Ah drink aboot a boattle a day... and so does everybody in ma tin hut."

"A BOATTLE A DAY?" Rita cried out. "It's a wonder youse are still staunin'! How can ye haud a boattle of whisky a day?"

"Oh, it's no' whisky we drink," Rasputin corrected.

"So, whit ur youse drinkin'?" Rita asked, curiously.

"Vantas," Rasputin said.

"VANTAS?" Rita said in disbelief.

"Aye, Vantas," Rasputin replied, a little embarrassed. "Ye know, they put a wee drap o' thick raspberry syrup intae a boattle, fill it up wi' watter and then stick in a tube frae an oxygen tank and fizz it up."

"Well, thank heavens for that!" Rita exclaimed, with relief. "Ah thought ye were spendin' yer money oan a boattle o' the hard stuff.. wastin' the money we should be savin' up for the bung."

"Naw, naw, Hen, Ah would never dae that," Rasputin said, squeezing her hand. "Ah just look forward tae the day when we have oor ain wee hoose wi' a room wi' cut-oot pictures o' Mickey Mouse and Donald Duck stuck on the wa's."

Rita sighed, "For oor wee wean?"

"Naw, for me," Rasputin said, "Ah always loved Donald Duck. Ma maw had ma room painted wi' Donald Duck because she knew how much Ah loved him. When Ah found oot he wisnae a real duck Ah gret ma eyes oot."

"Aw, whit a shame!" Rita said, pecking his cheek. "Whit age were ye?"

"Twenty-two," Rasputin said. "But ma maw made up for it. Wan Christmas she cooked a duck for oor dinner. Ah enjoyed that, it as jist like eatin' Donald."

"Ye were pleased, eh?" Rita said.

"Ah was!" Rasputin" said, "Ah just felt closer tae Donald than Ah ever was. An' Ah was just gled that Ah hadnae telt ma maw that Ah loved Mickey Mouse."

"Ach well, we a' have oor ain wee eccentricities. Ah'm just pleased that ye wurnae extravagant and that ye stuck tae drinkin' Vantas." Rita said.

"Aye, Ah was thinkin' aboot you and oor wee hoose," Rasputin said smiling. "Ah'll tell ye this, though. A' they gassy Vantas didnae dae oor stomaches any good. Ah mean, forty o' us, a' crammed intae the wan tin hut, a' sleepin' taegether, was nut very hygenic. A' that GAS! See if that tin hut had've been made o' canvas...we would've a' woke up in the moarnin' at thirty-thousand feet."

Rita laughed and squeezed his hand.

"Ye were awfu' brave the day...wi' that bomb!"

"Ah was lucky Ah was sittin' where Ah was when it went aff," Rasputin said, relief in his voice. "And we were lucky the blast went in a different direction frae your buildin'."

"Well, anywey, you were that brave, so ye were. You went doon there no' knowin' if ye were gonny get blown up or no'," Rita said proudly.

"Ah'm in that position every night in that tin hut," Rasputin said.

They stood silent for a moment, listening to Billy McGregor

playing the White Cliffs of Dover. It was Rita who broke the silence.

"Oh, Raspy , dae ye really think that wan day there could be Bluebirds over the White Cliffs of Dover?" she asked anxiously.

"Ah'm no' intae ornithology, Rita...except maybe ducks," Rasputin replied.

"Ah want ye tae promise me somethin'? Raspy," Rita said, a plea in her voice.

"Anyhin' ma wee lamb, you know that."

"Well," Rita said, twirling the button on Rasputin's tunic around her finger, "Ah want ye tae promise that if we are ever blessed by a wee wean wan day, you wull not insist on callin' him Rasputin."

"Ah think Ah can promise that, hen," Rasputin said, smiling. He was never too happy with the name himself. But his mother, being a very religious lady, wanted him called after a monk. In a way he was pleased because she was also into jungle pictures with a great affection for one of the leading actors in that field. He did not fancy himself being called Sabu Plunkett.

"Thank God!" Rita exclaimed .

"Ah'll go alang wi' your wishes, darlin'," Rasputin said. "If it's a wee lassie, you'll get first choice and, if it's a wee boy, the first choice is mine. That fair enough?"

"Fair enough!" Rita agreed.

"If it IS a wee boy, Ah'd call him efter ma favourite uncle, ma da's brother. He was at Glasgow University and took twenty examinations."

"Oh, Ah didnae know ye had a brainbox in the family, besides yerselel'!" Rita cried. "He must be the wan you got your genius frae. Whit was he finally, a lawyer, a doactor?"

"Naw, he failed every exam...flunked the lot!" Rasputin said, shaking his head, "He flunked every single wan and that's how he got his nickname."

"And whit was that?" Rita asked, narrowing her eyes suspiciously.

"Flunkit," Rasputin said.

"FLUNKIT?" Rita exploded and repeated, "FLUNKIT?"

"He was ma favourite uncle," Rasputin said with emphasis.

"Ah don't care if he was yer faither," Rita bellowed. "Nae

wean o' mine is gonny be called Flunkit, efter a dunce. Imagine him at his first day at school! 'Whit'ss yer name, son?' the teacher asks. 'Please Miss, Flunkit Plunkett', the wean says. Naw, naw, ye can forget that, Raspy. Besides that is nut a saint's name. Ah want a saint's name for ma wean and there is definitely NUT a Saint Flunkit."

"Dae Ah take it that ye don't like that name?" Rasputin asked questioningly.

"Ye take it right. Just call the wean Rasputin. It's better than Flunkit." Rita conceded.

"Ah canny see it happenin' anywey," Rasputin said sadly. "Ah mean we hivnae had much chance for to...er...you know."

Rita smiled. "There's always tomorrow," she said.

"That's no' much good if the Luftwaffe comes the night an' ye're blawed oot yer bed an' oot the windae."

"True enough!" Rita agreed. "But they don't come EVERY night," she said forcefully.

"True, true," Rasputin agreed. "So, let's get hame just in case we get a visit the night, In The Mood!"

"Are you on aboot that song again?" Rita said.

"No' this time, hen," Rasputin said, kissing her cheek. "C'mon"

They waited on for a few more dances before leaving. The full moon hung like a big yellow lantern and blue stars twinkled nervously against a black, velour sky.

Rita and Rasputin, hand-in-hand, walked down Bain Street and crossed London Road. They would pop into Peter Rossi's ice-cream shop, just opposite Well Street, and, if they were in luck, have a McCallum — a dollop of ice cream topped with a raspberry sauce. This had always been their favourite spot ever since their 'winching' days when they made it their rendevouz location. The girl behind the counter had their McCallum's all ready the minute she saw them entering the shop and sitting down at their favourite table. She switched the wireless on and Billy Ternant and his Orchestra's show had just begun on the Light Programme. The Ternant Big Band strings wafted through the shop before the brass blasted out with "Mairzy Doats and Dozy Doats", the ubiquitous mind-boggling song the wireless listeners could not escape.

They sat in silence for a while, just glad to be together and listening to the marvellous brass of the Ternant band. Ann Shelton, a sweetheart of the armed forces was guest singer and sang a song, "Stolen" from the German army and very popular with the allied armies...especially the British. The general population, too, had been seduced by Lily Marlene.

Rasputin and Rita stayed on in Peter Rossi's listening to the music and finally, waving goodnight to the counter girl, stepped out into the chill of the night. They shivered slightly but had only to cross the road and go down a short distance to number 27. They could see where they were going and managed to avoid the baffle walls.

Wullie and Annie had already retired to their respective bedrooms and, careful not to make a noise and waken them, the young couple tip-toed into their own bedroom and quietly closed the door.

Curdy McVey had collected the mortal remains of Missus Rosie McTaggart after requiem mass at St Alphonsus' church, in London Road, at the Barrows. With the shortage of petrol he had requested the 98-year-old woman's relatives follow the gleaming hearse on bikes donated by the Rapide Cycle Shop, of Stevenston Street. Some of the mourners had complained at this arrangement, especially the dead lady's twin sister. But Curdy was adamant. There was a war on and we all had to make sacrifices. He had suggested to the twin that she may not want to come back with them from St Peter's cemetery, at Dalbeth.

This did not go down at all well with the dear lady who gave him a tongue lashing only to be told to "get oan yer bike!

The twin would make the sacrifice but not for love of Rosie, she barely ever talked to her twin Not since that day, when Rosie stole her handsome, dashing Dragoon Cavalryman fiance. The discomfort of a bike was a small sacrifice to pay to see Rosie to her grave. The shortage of petrol affected all businesses and was a thorn in the side of Hector, Curdy McVey's undertaker employer. It had even been suggested one time when their monthly ration had run out before the next allowance was due, that a bus diver who had expired should be taken to his last resting place on the upstairs of a number forty-four Corporation bus. But this plan was rejected by the man's family and a wheelbarrow was used instead.

Curdy climbed into the driving seat and, glancing in his mirror to make sure that the bikers were all there behind and mounted, stuck his hand out of the window and moved off. He kept his eye on the trail behind him, especially the twin, for whom he had to stop now and again and order her off the pavement, particularly the sidewalk at the opposite side of the road, and get back into line. The wobbly lady cursed Curdy AND her sister who, even as a child, always WAS the favourite and got the best positions everywhere they went...from the theatre to the church. And, here she was again, travelling in style while SHE, the elder by two minutes, was astride a saddle that had all the comfort of a Gillette razor blade.

It was as the hearse and cycling cortege were passing Kirkpatrick Street, on the London Road, that things went wrong. Curdy's hearse spluttered to a stop. Frantically he rapped the fuel gauge with his knuckle but the pointer pointed contemptuously at EMPTY!

Curdy stepped down from the hearse and, walking to the back, held up his hand to halt the mourning cyclists. The bikes screeched to a stop...except for the McTaggart twin, who carried on right into Denholm's Bakery shop.

Curdy addressed the crowd. "Ah am sorry for to inform youse," he began, "that Ah have run out of petrol. This is because we ur at war and petrol is needed for oor tanks and things. Ma next allowance is nut until Monday of next week and so, it goes withoot saying, that Ah cannut keep this auld wumman in oor esteemed parlour until then for obvious reasons. The last time we did that a' the mice ran away. So, on behalf of Hector, ma boss, Ah apologise to youse for the inconvenience. Ah can only suggest that youse carry on cyclin' tae Dalbeth while Ah consider the best wey for tae get this auld wumman there tae her final plantin'."

There were murmurs of complaint and the twin, having been shown out of the bakers shop, laid into Curdy with her rolled up umbrella because of the inconvenience it was causing and NOT because of the ignominious way her sister was ending her final journey. Curdy watched the cyclists ride off up

London Road and, hauling the coffin out of the hearse, stood it vertically at the nearby tram stop where he stood at attention beside it.

A number nine 'caur' destined for Auchenshuggle would come along soon. This convenient tram passed the Dalbeth Cemetery and Curdy's desperate situation would be solved. He stood erect, his 'tile' hat, ebony black, glistening in the morning sunlight, his arm around the coffin to steady it as he did not want an accident which might result in a spillage.

Only one person might have enjoyed such a spectacle...and she was vanishing in the distance, in the wake of the receding thin black line.

Curdy wondered why passers-by were staring at him. Had none seen a man with a oak coffin standing at a 'caur' stop? Or, it could be, he smiled, how handsome he looked in his black frock coat and gleaming lum hat.

In the distance he saw the red tram heading his way and was glad he did not have long to wait for his transport.

Rita, hanging, hand on rail, from the platform couldn't believe her eyes. Was that a man standing at the next stop with an upright coffin by his side? She looked again and, indeed it was!

The 'caur' stopped and Curdy began to manhandle his charge across the few yards to the tram's platform. Steam began to come from Rita's ears.

"C'mon, get aff!" she bellowed. "You are nut bringin' that coaffin oan ma caur. So, aff!" She held up her hand. Curdy had managed to get the casket on to the first step of the 'caur'.

"Aw, Rita," he pleaded, "don't be rotten!"

Rita pushed her hand out further. "Deid boadies ur nut allowed oan public transport. It is the rules. AFF!"

"Aw, but Rita," Curdy pleaded. "Ah ran oot o' petrol and Ah've got for tae get this auld wumman tae Dalbeth where her faimily are already staunin' roon' the plantin spot."

"Aw, chuck it, Curdy," Rita said. "Ah've come oot withoot ma violin!"

"Yer caur passes Dalbeth," Curdy went on. "Just a few mair stoaps and Ah wull be alightin' for to take this dear auld wumman tae her new home."

"Ye could've borrowed a barra," Rita said.

"Aw, that widnae be dignified," Curdy protested. "Turnin' up pushin' her oan a barra."

"Ye think that arrivin' wi' her oan a number nine caur is dignified, dae ye?" Rita snapped.

"Aw, come on, hen?" Curdy said, almost weeping.

Rita remembered suddenly how Curdy had come to her recue and provided the transport for her wedding day. Of how he turned up with his hearse, albeit with the mortal remains of a Mrs McGinty in the back. But he got her to the church on time.

"A'right, she said at last, relenting. "Come on...but nae hymn singin'."

Curdy grinned and hauled the coffin on board and into the downstairs saloon where he stood, coffin upright beside him with a few other strap hanging passengers .

Rita put on her full authoritative voice. "Move up the caur there.. come on noo, make room for this deid boady."

Curdy stood beside a woman who was hanging to the strap with one hand and clutching a message beg with the other. Their eyes met. "Deid?" she said.

"Naw, Ah'm jist a bit peely-wally," Curdy said.

"Naw," the woman said screwing up her nose and nodding towards the coffin. "In there."

"Naw," Curdy said, "It's ma mother-in-law. Ah'm takin' her tae the Pavilion tae see Tommy Morgan."

"In THAT?" the woman said in disbelief.

"She likes a boax!" Curdy said without a smile.

A drunk man further along the car was desperately trying to light a broken cigarette that dangled from his lips. Rita's sharp eye zoomed in on him and she pushed her way along the car.

"No' YOU again!" she exclaimed.

"Aye, Ah think it's me," the drunk said.

"And ye're still smokin' that Pasha or ur ye still hivin' problems wi' yer bowels? Get that fag oot...whit a stink!" Rita was not amused.

"Ah am nut smokin' Pasha and that stink has got nothin' for tae dae wi' me. It's her," he nodded towards the coffin.

"How dare you, ya drunken wee swine," the lady with the message bag snapped.

"No' you, hen – her in the boax," the drunk said apologetically.

"She does nut smoke," Curdy said coming to his charge's defence.

"Take a good look at the coaffin," Rita said, "that's where ye end up wi' yer smokin'....especially Pasha. Right, noo, come oan, get aff." Rita began to steer the drunk to the back of the car where she belled the driver to stop and unceremoniously ejected the drunk.

The drunk, who had manage to retain his limp cigarette, stood swaying on the pavement and watched the car trundle on its way.

"Great, intit!" he slurred. "She throws me aff the caur 'cos Ah was bit stiff and she alows a bigger stiff than me tae stey oan." And with that and his last match failing to ignite the offending cigarette, he took it from his mouth and threw it on to the ground and, with anger, he ground it down with a shakey heel and staggered off.

Curdy, watching their route, was happy to see the 'caur' cross Springfield Road and clatter on up London Road and towards Dalbeth Cemetery.

Patting the coffin with affection he said, "Never mind, hen, ye might no' be gettin' a boax at the Pavilion. For you it's the GODS!"

"Right, this is near as you're gonny get," Rita said, belling the driver to stop.

Curdy manhandled Mrs Rosie McTaggart off the car and on to the pavement and Rita belled the driver to move off. Curdy stood at the stop, the coffin standing vertically at his side. He still had a hundred yards or so to transport his cargo to its destination and scratched his chin, wondering the best method. A wee boy whizzed past on roller skates and Curdy, for a fleeting moment, considered commandeering the wheels and laying on the box, thereby towing it along the pavement. But the wee boy was too quick and was gone in a flash.

The sounding of a horn made him look up and his face broke into a broad smile when he saw Cluckie Maguire's head hanging out of the cabin of his butcher's van. Cluckie and Curdy were related through drink and often met up at the Come Inn pub.

"Hivin' a bit o' trouble, pal?" Cluckie grinned.

"Ah ran oot o' petrol, Cluckie," Curdy said, "an' Ah've got a party o' mourners staunin' at Delbeth Cemetery, waitin' for tae pey their last respects tae this auld wumman."

"Stick her in the back o' the van," Cluckie nodded, "Ah've a delivery for tae make in Tollcroass Road if ye don't mind."

Curdy was only too pleased to accept Cluckie's offer and, rubbing his hands together, he hauled the coffin to the back of the van and, with Cluckie's help, loaded it aboard.

Cluckie tied the coffin vertically against the side of the van, between two large sides of beef.

"There!" he said, "that should dae the noo." He told Curdy to jump into the cab which he did and Cluckie turned up Helen Street and on to Tollcroass Road, where he stopped outside a butcher's shop.

Cluckie told Curdy to stay put and, jumping out, opened up the back doors of the van and took out the first side of beef - leaving the doors wide open as he vanished into the shop.

Two old pensioners, passing by, looked into the back of the van and, spotted the coffin standing there amongst the sides of beef. Their mouths fell open and they looked at each other in disbelief.

"Aw, Jessie, one said to the other, "wull ye look at that! Things must be worse than we thought!" and they shuffled on.

His business in the shop completed, Cluckie transported Curdy and his charge to Dalbeth where the mourners, bikes propped against headstones, stood, heads bowed around the grave. They looked up as the van approached up the path and their jaws dropped at the sign emblazoned on the van's side — "Cooked Meats", it said.

Rosie's twin raised her eyebrows. "Ah knew she'd end up in Hell!" she said with some satisfaction.

Curdy McVey, too, was satisfied as he made his way home that day, stopping at the Come Inn pub just to buck up his spirits. Rita's tram rolled into the Ruby Street depot. Her shift finished, she checked in her cash and ticket machine and was a bit annoyed that she had missed the lunch time Worker's Playtime concert that had been produced earlier that day. She was more annoyed when she learned that singer Robert

Wilson had topped the bill. But there was some consolation when he was told that the show would be broadcast on the BBC wireless at a later date.

Before heading home she sought out Wee Maisie Wilson and paid her weekly menage money. She was saving up just in case she might want to purchase a pram or other baby necessities at some later date. Maisie licked her pencil and noted the contribution in her little black book.

"That's three pounds twelve shullins ye've got tae date, Rita," Maisie said, "...Comin' oan, hen!"

Rita smiled and wondered when she would have to call it in. She left the depot on board a tram just going into service on the Rutherglen to Springburn route. The route would take it past her home. The driver, knowing Rita was aboard, slowed down as the car was passing Well Street and Rita, with a cheery wave, jumped off.

She was looking forward to the hot cup of tea she knew her mother would have waiting along with, if she was lucky, an abernethy biscuit. She stopped to look at a poster that had been pasted to the wall outside Mrs Mills' newsagent shop at the corner, in London Road.

The poster was issued by the Glasgow Corporation. It advised citizens how to avoid Enteric Fever and other diseases should the water supply system be damaged during a raid.

"If the water mains were badly damaged all water would have to be purified before drinking. You MUST boil the water," the poster advised, "OR purchase chlorinated Soda when ten drops must be added to each pint of water or two teaspoonsful to every pailful...then it should be allowed to stand for ten minutes before being used." A footnote said that the soda could be purchased at "your local chemist".

Luckily the local residents had escaped such a catastrophe and Rita hoped that they would never have cause to implement the advice. She carried on down the street and turned into number twenty seven. Nothing would deter her from that waiting cup of sweet tea.

Annie, as always, had the kettle boiling on the gas ring on top of the range where a comforting fire roared.

Greeting each other, Rita disappeared into her room and

76

peeled off the heavy green uniform and changed into a skirt. Entering the kitchen, she washed her hands at the sink and flopped down on a chair by the table. Wullie, licked his pencil and continued perusing his Noon Record and picking out his horses, running that day at Hamilton.

"Hello, hen!" he said, looking up. "Had a busy day?"

Annie poured the tea and Rita cupped her hands round the warm cup and sipped.

"Aw, ye've nae idea!" she said.

"That number nine route is always a busy wan," Annie stated authoritatively

"Ye don't know the hauf o' it, Mammy," Rita sighed. "Curdy McVey came on ma caur wi' a coaffin wi' a deid auld wumman in it."

"Curdy always DID go oot wi' dead certts," Wullie said with a wry grin.

"It's no' funny, Uncle Wullie," Rita said. "Whit if an inspector had come oan. Ah would've got intae trouble. You ur not allowed for to hiv deid boadies oan yer caur. And it's worse if they don't hiv a ticket."

"Well at least ye widnae have got any protests frae her if ye'd hiv thrown her aff," Wullie said cynically.

"Ye shouldnae hiv let him oan the caur," Annie said.

"Ah couldnae leave him staunin' in the street, could Ah?" Rita answered. "Ah mean he DID help me oot wi' transport at ma weddin'."

"Things are surely no' that bad that ye've tae get a caur tae yer ain funeral," Wullie commented dryly.

"His hearse had run oot o' petrol," Rita explained.

"Och, aye! It's this bloomin' war again!" Annie sighed.

Rasputin, boots shining black and brass buttons gleaming entered from the room carrying a suitcase.

"Well, time tae go!" he said.

Rita began to weep and threw her arms around him.

"It's no' fair!" she sobbed. "It feels like ye've jist been in the hoose ten minutes."

"The sooner Ah get back, the sooner this war wull end, hen," Rasputin said confidently.

"Whit's happeinin aboot yer gun that can shoot roon'

coarners, son?" Wullie asked keenly.

"Ah, it's still for tae be perfected," Rasputin' admitted.

Adding, "but the lads ur a' dead keen oan it and are hopin' it wull go intae production. Everywan o' them slapped ma back an' wished me luck the day we tried it oot for the first time."

"That's encouragin'," Wullie said. "They were obviously pleased wi' the results o' the test, eh?"

"Oh, aye," Rasputin said.

"Did it hit anythin'?" Wullie asked showing interest, himself being an old soldier.

"Oh aye, the sergeant major." Rasputin said.

"Was he a'right?" Wullie asked, raising his eyebrows.

"Aye," Rasputin said, "it was jist a flesh wound. The bullet went right through his heid and he said he would keep it as a souvenir."

"The bullet?" Annie said.

"His heid," Rasputin said. "And so he did. He kept the heid sayin' he was pleased tae be part of that very important experiment."

"It's good tae know ye're wanted," Wullie said drolly.

"Aye, he's wanted HERE!" Rita cried.

"Sorry, hen," Rasputin said, hugging her tightly, "but you're just in the same boat as thousands of other lassies. Ye can blame Hitler and his cohorts."

"Ah didnae know Hitler was a member o' the Co!" Annie said.

"Aye, well Ah've got a dividend for him, "Rasputin said, gritting his teeth.

"You tell 'em, son," Wullie said, shaking his hand.

"Let me come tae the station wi' ye, Raspy," Rita said, tiptoeing and looking pleadingly into his eyes.

Rasputin shook his head.

"Naw, hen," he said, "Ah don't like farewells at the station. We'll say cheerio here. Don't worry aboot anythin' — Ah'm only goin' intae Bomb Disposal, wan o' the maist dangerous units in the war where yer chance o' gettin' blawn up are rife."

"An' ye're tellin' me no' tae worry?" Rita wailed.

"Ah'll be wearin' armour," Rasputin said.

"It's nae good bein' Sir Lancelot, Raspy, it's no' bows an' arras ye're dealin' wi'," Rita bawled.

"Don't worry things'll go wi' a bang," Rasputin said and Rita bawled louder.

Annie pecked her son-in- law's cheek and Rasputin swept Rita into his arms and kissed her tenderly.

"Everythin' wull be fine, hen. When Ah'm oan ma knees attendin' tae that dangerous bomb that could go aff any minute blawin' me tae wee bits Ah'll be thinkin' of you."

Rita's wail could have been mistaken for an air-raid warning. With one final kiss Rasputin was gone.

Annie put a comforting arm around Rita's shoulder.

"He's a brave boy!" she said. Rita dabbed her eyes and stood erect.

"Well," she said with determination, "life goes on. Marriage is give an' take. A lot o' women hivnae got their man wi' them. It's the times we're livin' in," she said philosophically.

Everyone went quiet the stillness only to be shattered by Ina rushing in waving her left hand in the air.

"Hiv ye burnt yer finger?" Annie said with concern.

"Ma finger?" Rita blurted. "Naw, naw, there's nothin' wrang wi' ma finger...look." She held up her hand for all to see.

Wullie shrugged, "Wan finger's the same as any other," he said,"unless ye've got yer thumb grafted on!"

Ina kept her hand raised for all to see.

"Here, let's have a look," Annie said, examining Ina's hand.

Ina's engagement ring sparkled for a brief moment, catching the glow from the electric light bulb.

"Aw, Ina, it's lovely...look Rita, int that lovely?" Annie held up Ina's hand. Rita burst into tears and ran from the room, throwing herself on top of her bed sobbing bitterly Ina looked at Annie questioningly.

"Jist leave her," Annie said. "Rasputin's gone back tae his barracks in England and she's upset."

"Aw, Ah'm sorry, Annie," Ina said sadly. "Ah picked the wrang time tae come in."

"You wurnae tae know," Annie said softly. "C'mon, noo, well, that's it offical, eh?"

"Aye, official," Ina said, holding her hand out and twisting it to and fro for all to admire. "Charlie gave me it the day and we've named the big day."

"Oh, when?" Annie said excitedly.

"Two weeks the morra," Ina twittered.

"Aw, that's lovely, Ina...int it, Wullie?"

Wullie ruffled his newspaper and shrugged.

"Congratulations, hen!" Annie said, pecking Ina's cheek, "Ah'm sure Rita wull gie ye her paras...er... weddin' dress if ye want it."

Ina shook her head. "Aw, thanks a lot, Annie. But Ah'm a wee bit aulder than Rita..."

"A BIG bit," Wullie interrupted.

Annie scowled and Ina ignored Wullie's rudeness.

"Ah think Ah'll get merried in a suit," Ina said.

"Ah'll lend ye wan o' ma auld wans," Wullie volunteered.

Ina shook her head in despair at Wullie's facetiousness and, ignoring him, went on, "Ah'm gonny go ower tae Madame Ashe's, in Gorbals Street, for a nice powder-blue suit...IF Ah can get enough clothing coupons. Ah'll need tae try and find some!"

"Ah wish Ah could help ye, Ina," Annie said, "but Ah've used up ma quota, gettin' oor Rita a trousseau."

"There's only wan man in the whole o' the Calton can help ye here, hen!" Wullie said, standing full erect and putting his hand on his heart in a reverential gesture.

"And who's that?" Ina inquired.

"Fingers McGeachie," Wullie said, with obvious deep admiration.

Ina and Annie together gave a whoop of delight. "Of coorse," they cried. "Fingers can put his haun' on ANYTHIN'!"

"Except dugs's crap," Wullie reminded them.

It was with deep affection that Annie thought of Fingers McGeachie. She appreciated how he acquired a pig for Rita's wedding and, when the ever watching Erchie McPherson 'recaptured' the porker, Fingers went out of his way to find alternative fayre for the wedding reception.

"He'll no' need ta get us any food!" Ina said.

"Ah don't need any food coupons for the weddin'," she went

on, "Ah've been savin' ma food coupons up... Ah hivnae been eatin' the same since ma da' died."

"Ye'd never know it," Wullie said dryly.

Ina turned on him. "Ur you suggestin' Ah'm fat or somethin' That Ah'm a big eater?" she demanded.

"Ah never said that," Wullie said. "But if Ah was Charlie Ah widnae let ye near ma hoarse."

"You ur incorrigible," Ina sniped. Then, turning to Annie, went on, "Ah'll no' need tae worry aboot drink. We'll have plenty!"

"Aye, we'll be sittin' drinkin' bloody mulk a' night," Wullie said snidely.

"Naw, naw," Ina said, "Charlie is well in wi' Jimmy Smith at the 'Come Inn' pub."

"Oh! It's a' very excitin', int it?" Annie enthused.

Rita pecked Ina on the cheek. "Ah'm right happy for ye, Ina."

"Thanks, Rita," Ina said, "Ah thought it would never happen!"

"Aye, well everythin' comes to those who wait," Rita said, adding, "Well, Ah think Ah'll have forty winks." And Rita vanished into her room.

Annie's mind was on clothes coupons.

"Aye, well, we'll have tae see aboot they clothing coupons," she said.

Wullie got up. "Aye, well, Ah'm goin' oot for a donner," he said, "Ah'll try and arrange for to see Fingers. Leave it wi' me."

Ina pecked his cheek. "Thanks, Wullie, ye're a sport!" she said.

Wullie grunted. "Aye... er...aye," he stammered and left the room.

Annie heard the outside door closing and, turning to Ina, said, "Wullie wull fix things, Ina, don't worry. Right, noo, let's you an' me have a wee cuppa tea, eh?"

Ina leaned back on her chair and thought how lucky she was to have a neighbour like Annie and how everything was falling into place. She hoped that she was doing the 'right thing'. For, deep down, she still had that wee feeling for Wullie McSorley - the very man who was out trying to make her wedding day a big success. Her thoughts were interrupted by Annie placing the hot cup of tea in front of her.

"Drink up, hen," Annie said, "Ye're in yer aunties!"

Yes, Ina thought as she sipped the sweet tea, how fortunate she was. Annie was, indeed, much closer to her than any of her aunts.

Placing her cup on to the saucer, Ina looked across at Annie. "Annie," she said, slowly, "Ah wonder if ye would do me a wee favour?"

Annie replaced her own cup and looked up with interest.

"Of coorse, Ina, anythin'," she said.

"Would ye be ma best maid?" Ina said, almost shyly.

"Ah'd be honoured, Ina," Annie said with a broad smile.

"Ye're ma best, true freen', Annie," Ina said quietly.

Annie came round the table and kissed Ina lightly on the cheek.

"God bless ye, hen!" she said, feeling a tear coming to her eye.

"And," Ina went on, "D'ye think Wullie would gie me away?" she asked hopefully.

"Ye don't think auld Jake would mind?" Annie asked, thinking of how Wullie lost Ina's father's ashes down the sink.

Ina pooh-poohed the suggestion.

"That's a' watter under the bridge," she said... "as well as ma da' tae!"

They both burst out laughing and Annie was glad to see that Ina was not dwelling on the catastrophe.

Wullie made straight for the 'Come Inn' pub, in Stevenston Street and was greeted by Jimmy Smith, the barman.

"Usual, Wullie?" Jimmy inquired.

Wullie nodded and Jimmy Smith poured out a pint of McEwans heavy and pushing over to Wullie, said: "Ye're no' usually in here at this time, Wullie. Did Annie throw ye oot?"

Wullie drew a 'she widnae dare' look.

"Naw, it is imperative that Ah contact Fingers McGeachie, Jimmy," he said.

"Fingers?" Jimmy said, raising his eyebrows. "Ah believe he's lyin' low the noo... because of the disappearance of hauf-a-ton o' sugar frae the City Chambers' kitchen."

"Fingers did THAT?" Wullie said with some admiration.

"He did," Jimmy said, "An' Ah'll tell ye this, Wullie, it's amazin' the number o' auld pensioners goin' aroon here wi' smiles oan their faces... SWEET smiles, ye might say." Jimmy laughed loudly and Wullie joined in.

"He's some man!" Wullie exclaimed. "And Ah must see him as soon as possible."

"Ah'll keep ma eye oot for him an' gie him yer message, Wullie," Jimmy Smith said.

"Aye, a'right, Jimmy," Wullie said and, finishing off his drink, ambled towards the door."

Ina had gone when Wullie arrived back at the house. He flopped on to a chair at the table and Annie poured out two large glasses of El Dorado wine.

Wullie sipped and, satisfied, leaned back on the chair.

Annie raised her glass

"Tae Ina an' Charlie," she said.

Wullie remained silent.

"May they find happiness," Annie added and, again, Wullie said nothing.

"Ina wants you for to gie her away," Annie said, "wull ye dae that?"

Wullie sighed, "Well, seein' as Ah loast her faither doon the plughole, it's the least Ah can dae," he said.

"It's gonny break your heart walkin' doon the aisle wi' Ina oan yer airm, intit?" Annie said with conviction.

"Naw it wullnae!" Wullie snapped.

"Ye've only yersel' tae blame," Annie said, driving the nail in harder. "Ye've loast a lovely lassie...a lovely wife that would've made ye happy."

"Ach, ye're haverin'!" Wullie snarled.

"Am Ah?" Annie retorted, "Ye canny kid me! That's a' banter between you an' Ina. Ye're just thrawn, Wullie, And yer stubbornness has loast ye a loat o' happiness. Ah think Ina feels she's gettin' oan a bit and, wi' you ignoring a' her hints and advances, she took on Charlie Gallagher on the rebound...although Ah dae think she likes him. He seems a nice fella!"

"Ah well," Wullie said philosophically, "that's life!"

Wullie poured out two more glasses of El Dorado.

"Here," he said to Annie, "Here's tae US!"

Annie took the drink and walked over to the wireless.

"Let's cheer oorsel's up," she aid, switching it on.

A female singer blasted out the popular song, 'Who's Sorry Now'.

Wullie spluttered on his drink and, marching across the room, switched the wireless off with a contemptuous flick."

Wullie arose to the sun streaming in the bedroom window. Rita had already left for work and, after washing under the brass, swan-necked cold tap at the sink, Wullie had a cup of tea and a slice of toast. Putting his overcoat on, he said to Annie, "Ah'm just goin' for a wee walk seein' it's a nice day."

Wullie hesitated at the closemouth, trying to decided which way to go. Making his mind up, he turned into London Road and headed towards Bridgeton Cross. He turned up into Landressy Street and entered the public library where he spent the next hour browsing through some of the books that took his fancy. The sun was still shining brightly as he emerged from the imposing red-stone building and, turning right, he came to Bridgeton Cross itself where he sat on a bench under the 'umbrella' a landmark and where many pensioners met, under the clock, for chat or just to sit and watch the world go by. They saw the green cars going east up Main Street to Rutherglen and the red cars heading up Dalmarnock Road to Burnside or up London Road to Auchenshuggle and Carmyle. The yellow cars, turning at James' Street, going south to Bellahouston. It seemed the whole world passed by at Bridgeton Cross. To his right was the Olympia Cinema, the most luxurious picture hall in the East End.

After a while Wullie got up and headed down James' Street and on to Greenhead Street where he turned right and began to walk west through Glasgow Green. He stood and eyed the imposing building of Templeton's Carpet factory. For all the world it resembles a caliph's Baghdad palace, designed in brightly coloured tiles in exotic patterns. Standing looking at it he could almost hear the music of 'The Desert Song'. Wullie walked on and saw the football pitches that brought back boyhood memories.

Much of the Green had been dug up and air-raid shelters installed deep under ground. He shook his had sadly with the thought that the war he fought in 1914 was supposed to be the war that ended all wars. And here we were again fighting each other. Where these dug out holes were the sanctuaries for sleepy children and worn out mothers whose rest had been disturbed by the ruthless Luftwaffe. He walked on and saw the part of the public park where the gang wars of the old days took place. Where the San Toi from Calton and the Norman Conks or Billy Boys, from Bridgeton would meet and battle it out. That was during the depression days of the late Twenties and early Thirties. Now, most of those same gang members were either old men sitting at places like the Umbrella, remembering old times, or were young enough to be conscripted and were now fighting a REAL battle. The battle for freedom and oppression. If they go into battle with the spirit they had down at Glasgow Green, we were bound to win this war, Wullie reflected with a wry smile.

He walked on and turned into the People's Palace, a museum which held for Wullie many memories, too, from his boyhood. He remembered holding on to his father's hand as his dad pointed out the bright uniforms of the Scottish regiments of wars gone by. Swords, sabres and muskets of yore fired a boy's imagination. He would see himself at the Charge of the Light Brigade, the Battle of Waterloo and in the daring exploits of the reivers.

Leaving the imposing building, he turned and entered the large adjacent , large greenhouse. The heat him as soon as he entered and the sweet smell of the flora hit his nostrils. He marvelled at the spiky cacti from Arizona, the exotic flowers from around the world, Of beautiful orchids, red roses...and white ones, too. Of palms and sweet smelling hyacinths. This was the perfume of Eden and Wullie was at peace and his appreciation for those who brought this paradise to Glasgow's East End welled up in his heart. He left the exotic behind and crossed busy London Road and headed down towards 'The Barras'. The market would be open, today being Saturday. He joined the crowd gathered round 'Irish Paddy', who was bound up tightly in chains and strait jacket and was endeavouring, Houdini fashion, to extricate himself...which he did to great applause.. Wullie joined in throwing coins into the Irishman's "bunnet" that lay on the ground. Wullie strolled on, into Gallowgate and up towards Bain Square. He stopped at the Oyster Bar and purchased a bag of 'wulks', making sure the required pin was attached to the brown poke. He ate as he walked. Crossing the children's playground, he turned down Well Street, stopping at the Come Inn pub where Jimmy Smith greeted him with the news that Fingers McGeachie had received his message and would be calling at number 27 shortly. Wullie thanked him, offered Jimmy a 'wulk' which he refused and then headed on home.

Annie, her coat on, and her message bag on her arm, was about to leave when Wullie got in.

"Ah'm just goin' up tae Galbraiths tae see if anythin's come in," she said.

"Aye, right!" Wullie said, hanging his coat behind the door.

"Ah, Annie, ye get mair like Betty Grable every day!"

Annie giggled as Finger McGeachie swept her off her feet.

"Oh, Fingers McGeachie!" Annie blushed," Ah never heard ye comin' up the stairs."

Fingers, tall and well dressed, with a small 'Ronald Coleman' moustache, laughed. "The quiet man, that's me," he said with a chuckle. "Maybe they should call me 'Toes', eh?"

Wullie was delighted that Fingers had answered his summons.

"Come in, Fingers, come in," Wullie said.

Fingers had left a brown paper bag down before he gave Annie a whirl. He retrieved it and going into the house, handed it to Annie.

"Here, hen," he said, "that's for you."

Annie's brows shot up.

"For ME?" she said, with some excitement in her voice.

Fingers nodded.

"For you, hen," he said.

Annie looked into the bag and let out a whoop of delight. Putting her arm in, she pulled out the contents.

"HAUF-A-DOZEN EGGS!!" Annie's delight could be heard all over the building.

Aw, Fingers, ye're a pet," Annie said, pecking his cheek, "Wherever dis ye get them?"

"Ah know a friendly hen," Fingers said with a twinkle in his eye.

"C'mon," Annie said, playfully digging his ribs, " less o' yer kiddin'."

"Naw, it's right enough," Fingers said, "Annie, would Ah lie?" Fingers put on an expression of mock hurt. "Ah DID get them frae a friendly hen, honest. Ah just happened for to be passin' by that wee dairy roon' the coarner an' ma eye caught the wee blonde behind the coonter...a wee stoater! Anywey, in Ah went and went straight up tae her an' said, "You look friendly, hen! Would ye like for tae accompany me tae the Dennistoun Palais on Setturday night?"

"How could she possible refuse an approach like that?" Annie laughed.

"Dead right, hen," Fingers said, "So right away she gave me them eggs."

Fingers straightened his tie and breathed on his fingernails.

Annie and Wullie both laughed at his cheek.

"Oh, ye're an awfu' man, Fingers. But look here, Ah'll have tae run Ah'll leave you two tae get oan wi' yer business."

Annie left with a cheery wave and Wullie, turning to Fingers, said, "Come away in, Fingers, sit ye doon."

Fingers sat at the table and Wullie took the chair opposite.

"Want a drink of El Dorado?" Wullie said, holding up the bottle.

Fingers grimaced. "Na, naw, Ah'n strictly a whisky man, Wullie, you should know that." It was almost a rebuke.

"Sorry Ah canny help ye there," Wullie said.

"Naw, but Ah can help you," Fingers said, producing a half bottle of Johnny Walker from his jacket pocket. Wullie's eyes lit up and Fingers poured ample proportions into the glasses Wullie offered.

Both men took a large gulp and Wullie smacked his lips with satisfaction.

"Right," Fingers said, "let's get doon tae buiness. Jimmy Smith telt me ye wanted for to see me urgently?"

Wullie nodded.

"Aye, Fingers," he began, "there's a wee favour Ah want tae ask ye, Fingers...two, in fact."

Fingers leaned back, put his fingertips together steeple fashion and said, "Well, Wullie," he said, "ye know ma philosophy...if Ah can help somebody as Ah pass along...naebody lingers when they ask a favour frae Fingers..."

"True enough, Fingers, or 'Jist ask McGeachie, if there's somethin' you seekie' Wullie laughed.

"Ah like that, Wullie, Ah like that!", Fingers said smiling.

"Aye, well it IS true. You are known as the Robin Hood of the Calton.

Fingers pooh-poohed the idea with a wave of the hand.

"Noo, c'mon, tell me whit it is ye want," he said.

"Well," Wullie began, "ma first request is oan behalf o' Ina McLatchie."

"Ah, dear Ina...whose faither was a well-known thespian,!" Fingers said in a flamboyant tone.

"Ah didnae know he was a thespian," Wullie said, "Ah always thought it was jist women that could be wan o' them. He wisnae a wumman, Ina's faither, was he?"

"Ah THESPIAN, Wullie, is somebody who treads the boards," Fingers said with some impatience.

"Well, that would be right enough!" Wullie said, "Ah used tae hear him walkin' up an' doon a' night, treadin' the boards...wonderin' if he should brave tha cauld an' go doon tae the lavvy...an' he always did."

"Naw, ye've got it wrang, Wullie." Fingers said. "It's nothin' tae dae wi' folk wantin' tae go tae the lavvy. A thespian is an ACTOR.

"Oh!" Wullie exclaimed," Aye, that's right, he was wance in a film wi' Rin-Tin-Tin, the great American dug actor."

"Did he get an Oscar?" Fingers asked.

"Naw, he got distemper," Wullie said. "Even jist before he died, if he had a a heidache, he never took an Askit like the rest o' us, He took a Bob Martin's."

Fingers laughed. "Aye, a'right, Wullie, Noo, whit's Ina's problem?"

"Ina's gettin' married," Wullie said a note of bitterness in his tone.

"Pigs are oot, Ah'm afraid," Fingers said. Whit aboot a jersey?"

Wullie shook his head. "Naw," he said, "Ah canny see her walkin' doon the aisle in her nice froak an' wearin' a jersey."

"Naw, naw!" Fingers cried, "No' a Jersey jersey...a COO jersey. Ah have reason for to believe that a herd is comin' this weye for the nutrition of the American sojers who are billeted at the Beresford Hotel. They wull be rounded up and pastured somewhere in the Campsie Fells."

"It's nothin' like that she wants, Fingers," Wullie said, "But if there happens tae be a stray coo?"

Fingers shook his head. "Nut necessary, Wullie," he said, "If the Yanks know that Auld Mr McLatchie wance acted in a film wi' Rin-Tin-Tin, the great dug actor frae Hollywood, Ah'm sure they would gladly donate a spare coo. It would nut be necessary for me to don ma black cowboy hat and swing ma lassoo."

"Aye, well, the situation does NUT arise", Wullie said, "In fact the man Ina is mairryin' is in the coo trade himsel'.. he's a Mulkman. Her dire need is for some clothin' coupons for to outfit hersel' for the big day."

"Are we no' better capturin' another Luftwaffe parachutist for to acquire his silken parachute for the use of?"

"Naw, that's too dicey, Fingers," Wullie commented.

"In fact she wants tae get married in a suit for to be purchased at Madame Ashe's, in Gorbals Street."

Fingers' eyes lit up. "Ah! Madame Ashe's! An auld flame o' mine! Tell Ina her troubles are over. Here..."

Fingers produced a book of clothing coupons and handed it to Wullie.

"Take ma coupons, Wullie!"

"Aw, Fingers, that's helluva generous o' ye," Wullie cried in admiration.

Fingers shrugged. "Wullie, when dae AH need claeths coupons, eh? Ah can get anyhin' Ah want, anytime," he said proudly.

"Still," Wullie said, "it's still good o' ye!"

"Naw, naw, Wullie." Fingers said, holding up his hand, "the only thing Ah require right noo is a boiler suit."

"Aw, come aff it, Fingers!" Wullie cried, "Whit would YOU dae wi' a boiler suit, eh?" The thought, to Wullie's mind, was absolutely ridiculous.

"No' for ME, Wullie, "Fingers said with horror, "For a boiler Ah know."

Wullie laughed loudly. "Ye're a' heart, Fingers!" Wullie said.

"Wan thing, Wullie," Fingers said, "Don't tell Ina Ah gave ye ma ain coupons...Ah mean Ah've got ma reputation for to consider.."

Wullie nodded, he understood. "It's oor secret, Fingers," he said, tapping the side of his nose.

"But, ye said ye had TWO favours tae ask, Wullie?" Fingers said, narrowing his eyes.

"Aye, right enough," Wullie said. "The other favour's for masel'."

"For you, anythin', Wullie," Fingers said with sincerity.

Before Wullie could confide in him the door burst open and a breathless Curdy McVey rushed in.

"Aw, Fingers," he cried, "Am Ah gled tae see you!" And, turning to Wullie, he said apologetically, "Ah'm sorry for bargin' in like that, Wullie, but Jimmy Smith telt me Fingers was up here And it is infindutably necessary that Ah see him."

Wullie dismissed the apology with a wave.

"Forget it, Curdy!" he said.

"Aw, thanks, Wullie, "Curdy cried.

"Whit's yer problem, Curdy?" Fingers asked, wondering what an undertaker wanted with HIM.

"You ur the only man in this world that can solve ma problem except maybe Al Capone," Curdy said.

Wullie rose and put a dining chair at Curdy's disposal.

"Sit doon, Curdy," Wullie said, "Take yer problem aff yer feet."

Curdy thanked Wullie and sat down and breathed heavily.

"Right, then?" Fingers said, raising his brows.

"WAIT!" Wullie said, raising his hand. He lifted the half bottle and looked questioningly at Fingers.

Fingers nodded and Wullie topped up three large glasses.

"Right, noo!" Fingers said, "So whit's YOUR problem, Curdy?"

Curdy took a good swig of his drink and gave a satisfactory belch.

"Petrol!" he said.

"Hey, the whisky's no' as bad as that!" Fingers retorted.

"Naw," Curdy said, "That's ma problem, PETROL. We've ran oot o' oor petrol ration and we're no' due any mair for two weeks."

"There's an easy solution tae that problem," Fingers said.

"An' whit's that?" Curdy asked raising his eyebrows.

"Jist tell yer customers tae hing oan an' no' tae die for a couple of weeks," Fingers said, winking at Wullie.

"Aw, very funny, Fingers," Curdy cried. "Ah've already got hauf-a-dozen boadies waiting for to go to their final restin' place."

Curdy was near to tears.

"That bad is it?" Fingers said.

"Oh, aye, it's that bad," Curdy agreed.

"Ah'm daein' a good deal in gas masks the noo," Fingers said.

"Naw, they're deid. They don't need gas masks," Curdy cried.

"Ah meant for yersel'? "Fingers said. "Ah mean, the place must be stinkin'!"

"It's like a gorgonzola factory," Curdy admitted.

"Well, we canny have that," Fingers said. "So, don't worry Curdy. Yer problem is solved."

Curdy couldn't believe his ears. It was as easy as that!

"Y...ye mean ye can help me oot?" he gasped.

"Curdy, you be here in this hoose at nine o'cloack the night and Ah'll bring ye yer petrol."

"Aw...aw ye're a live saver, Fingers!" Curdy blurted.

"A death saver ye mean," Fingers laughed.

Curdy laughed nervously.

"Whit can Ah dae tae thank ye, Fingers?" he said.

"Ye can gie me a free funeral when the time comes," Fingers said with a shiver.

"It'll me ma pleasure." Curdy said, quickly adding, if ye see whit Ah mean!" Fingers laughed.

"Aye, Ah see whit ye mean," he said.

"Ah'll see ye get a real, widden coaffin, Fingers," Curdy said proudly, " bane of that veneer crap for you!"

"Good!" Fingers said, "that'll gie a good impression tae who-ever meets me at the other side."

"Where dae ye think ye're goin', Fingers?" Wullie said, wondering at the reply.

Fingers shrugged:

"Ah don't know," he said, "but bury me in an asbestos suit." They all laughed.

"An' ye think ye'll have ma petrol for me the night?" Curdy said in disbelief.

"Nae doot aboot it!" Fingers said smugly, "The Home Guard owe me a favour ever since Ah supplied them wi' bicycle pumps."

"Whit did they want THEM for?" Curdy asked.

"For tae blaw up the Germans, whit else?" Fingers grinned.

Curdy missed the gag. "Have ye got a connection at the Home Guards' depot?" he haltingly asked

"Ah hiv!" Fingers said assuredly.

"An officer?" Curdy asked with a devilish glint in his eye.

"Ma connection is nut an officer," he said. "It is a rubber tube." he winked at Wullie who grinned. They all laughed and Fingers poured out three more whiskies.

"There was somethin' else you wanted, Wullie, that right?" he said.

Wullie felt embarrassed. Cupping his hand over Fingers' ear he whispered something to him. "Excuse ma ignorance, Curdy," he apologised, "but this is very personal."

"Think nothin' aboot it," Curdy said with a dismissive wave.

"Consider it done, Wullie," Fingers said.

"Aw, God bless ye, Fingers," Wullie said, smiling broadly.

"If he DOES, Ah'll no' need that asbestos suit, wull AH?" Fingers laughed with the other pair joining in.

Ina and Annie walked along to Bridgeton Cross where they caught a number 7 yellow car heading for Bellahouston.

Ina was excited. Fingers McGeachie was her hero. She wondered where he acquired the clothing coupons that were nestling in her handbag? But she was excited and was delighted when Annie offered to accompany her to Madame Ashe's shop, in Gorbals Street.

It seemed no time at all until they were alighting at Gorbals Cross. As the crossed the road Annie tugged at Ina's sleeve.

"Look!" she said.

"Whit? Whit is it?" Ina asked worriedly.

"That shoap ower there," Annie nodded," look at the queue ootside....c'mon."

Annie pulled Ina forward and they both joined up at the end of the queue.

"Whit's the queue for?" Annie asked the woman at the end of the queue.

The woman shrugged. "Hivnae a clue," she said, "but Ah heard somebody mention EGGS."

"EGGS?" Annie said, "Oh, we'll jist wait, then."

Queues were commonplace and any line-up outside a shop meant that some commodity hard to get was available.

The two women stood 'blethering' for what seemed an eternity A little man with a bushy moustache was taking charge of things at the head of the queue.

"Next two," he would say in an authoritative voice, ushering the next couple in the queue into the shop.

Annie would step out now and then and focus on the head of the queue, watching for customers leaving the shop to see if she could spot hat they had purchased. But it was hopeless! Not one single customer showed anything that would give her a clue. In fact most of them left the shop with long, gloomy faces.

"Ask doon the line whit exacytly it is they're sellin' in that shoap," she asked the woman in front. The woman nodded and asked the lady in front of her, "Whit is it they're sellin'?" And so it went on right down the line. The answer came back up the line a few minutes later.

"Puddin' eggs," the woman in front of Annie said.

"Puddin' Eggs?" Annie queried. "Whit's that?"

The woman shrugged.

"Whit dae ye think that is, Ina?" Annie said, puzzled.

"Must be eggs for makin' puddin's," she said, "Like Creamola an' that."

But Annie was not satisfied. "An egg's an egg, Ina," she said.

93

"How can a hen tell whit kind o' egg it's gonny lay? Does it say tae its man, 'Hey Wullie, Ah think Ah'll lay a couple o' puddin' eggs the day...or bilin' eggs, or fryin' eggs'."

"Maybe there's weys they can tell," Ina said.

"We'll hing oan anywey," Annie said, "Ah'm sure puddin' eggs or no', they can still be biled."

Ina and Annie waited for twenty minutes in the queue. People seemed to spend little time in the shop. In and out in a jiffy.

Suddenly Ina and Annie were face to face with the little man with the big moustache.

"Right, next," the man said and Ina and Annie found themselves in front of a large, gaunt man behind the counter.

"How many dae ye want?" he asked, peering under heavy set eyebrows.

"As much as Ah can get," Annie said. "Three dozen would be very welcome."

"THREE DOZEN?" the man nearly had a fit.

"Well, theres three o' us in the hoose," Annie said, "so that would gie us a dozen each."

"Naw, naw,"the man said sternly, "Jist two tae a household,"

"A'right", Annie said, "two dozen wull jist have tae dae."

"Ah'm no' talkin' aboot two DOZEN," the man said, "Ah am talkin' aboot TWO...wan, two," he said, holding up two fingers.

"TWO?" Annie said in disbelief. "TWO?" That means wan o' us wull have tae dae withoot."

"Ye're no' sorry aboot that, ur ye?" the man said.

"Of coorse Ah am," Annie said. "Ah'll jist gie wan o' mine."

"And whit wull you dae for gettin' around?" the man asked with some concern

"Whit dae ye mean?" Annie asked, knitting her brows.

"It's unusual for three o' ye in the wan hoose tae hiv the same disability." the thin man said.

"Whit disability?" Annie cried. "And whit's that got tae dae wi' me buyin' puddin' eggs?"

"Whit ur ye talkin' aboot, hen?" the man cried. "Ah'm no' sellin' puddin' eggs, Ah am sellin' Wooden Legs,"

"It looks like the message got loast in transmission," Annie sighed. "But maybe Ah SHOULD take a couple."

"Don't be daft!" Ina said, "whit would ye want them for?"

"For Wullie," Annie said. "Some Setturday nights he comes hame...legless."

The two women laughed loudly and left the shop....guffawing to the waiting queue.

They turned into Gorbals Street and it was with excitement that Ina entered Madame Ashe's Fashion Boutique."

"Ah want a two-piece suit in powder blue," Ina told the young girl assistant.

"Is the garment for a special occasion madame is attending?" the girl asked.

Ina blushed. "Aye," she said shyly, "ma weddin"

"Ooh! congratulations," the girl cooed. "And what will Madame's 'groom be wearing – kilt or morning suit?"

"Ah'm no' sure," Ina said. "He might well wear his uniform."

At the word uniform' the girl's arms flew up and she gave a whoop of joy. "Ah, we love to give the brides of our gallant men special treatment...under the counter, you might say."

"That's very nice o' ye," Ina twittered.

The girl vanished and returned with a powder blue suit...in gaberdine.

Ina's eyes widened.

"This is the latest," the girl said, "and just madame's size, too - eighteen."

"Ah jist take a sixteen," Ina said haughtily.

"My misatake, madame," the girld said apologetically. "We do have a sixteen. I'll fetch it."

The girl vanished through a door and Ina looked at Annie. "Whit dae ye think o' the cheek o' that?" she said, annoyed.

Annie laughed, "Ach she's only a wee lassie," she said in way of mitigation.

The girl was back immediately and ushered Ina into a changing room with the replaced garment. Annie's eyes swept around the shop, enjoying the fashions and display. Ina emerged from the changing room, stood in front of Annie and did a twirl.

"Da-Da!" she sang in mock fanfare.

95

"Aw, Ina, ye look lovely, hen. It's jist you!" Annie said with admiration.

Ina blushed. The girls assistant agreed with Annie and poured out all the adjectives ending with:

"You could only enhance your 'groom's uniform, Madame. "he will be very proud of you. What colour is HIS uniform?"

"White," Ina said.

"Perfect!" the girl cooed. "A naval officer?"

"Naw, he's a milkman," Ina said.

"Oh!" the salesgirl said, her hand coming up to her mouth.

"Ah'll take it," Ina said, "Dae ye take Provident Cheques?"

Before the girl could answer, Annie interrupted.

"Nae need!" she said, "We'll pey cash!"

Ina turned to Annie, "Annie, whit are ye sayin'?" she asked, knitting her brows.

"Ina, Wullie slipped me a tenner before we left the hoose," she said, "It's his weddin' present tae ye."

"Aw, Annie, Ah canny accept a' that," Ina said.

"Look, Ina," Annie said reassuringly, "Wullie has always been a bachelor and he gets his army pension and he's no' short of a few bob although he's always pleadin' poverty. So you take it wi' his blessin'."

"Aw thanks, Annie". He's a wee gem...despite his pot shots at me."

Annie laughed, "Ach don't let it bother ye," she said, "it's just his wey."

Ina paid over the money and handed the girl her clothing coupons. Half-an-hour later the happy pair left the shop and were lucky to wait just a few minutes at the car stop when a number seven yellow car heading for Riddrie came along. They alighted at the foot of Abercromby Street and walked the rest of the way along London Road.

"C'mon, we'll go intae Rossi's for a McCallum tae celebrate," Annie prompted.

They sat and talked and Annie said she, "May pay Madame Ashe's a visit masel'." They stayed in Rossi's for about twenty minutes before crossing the road and heading home.

Ina McLatchie was very pleased with her day!

FIVE

FINGERS McGEACHIE LOADED THE FOUR CANS OF PETROL, EACH holding five gallons, on to a wheelbarrow he had acquired. It was dark now, the blackout being in full force. And Fingers was glad! For he could avoid detection as he pushed the barrow through the streets towards number 27 Well Street.

It was when he turned the corner from Stevenston Street into Well Street, he heard that familiar voice that made him stop in his tracks.

"Hello! Hello! Hello! and whit have we here, eh?" Erchie McPherson stepped out of the doorway of Mary Welsh's sweetie shop. His nose began to twitch and twitched even harder as he approached the wheelbarrow.

"Ah smell..." he started.

"Aye, no' half," Fingers said.

Erchie was elated. At last he had caught Fingers McGeachie red-handed.

"Whit's a' this then, eh?" he said almost jovially

"Good evenin', Erchie," Fingers said.

"Special Constable McPherson tae you, McGeachie," Erchie snapped.

"Aye..er, right," Fingers mumbled.

"This," Erchie said sternly, pointing towards the barrow," is cans of petrol pinched from Ah know nut where...but PINCHED never the less!"

"It's mine!" Fingers said.

"You hivnae got a motor car, McGeachie," Erchie snapped.

"Ah've got a lighter," Fingers snapped back

"A lighter?" Erchie said, shaking his head.

"Aye, an' Ah always like for tae cairry some spare petrol wi' me in case it runs dry."

Erchie laughed a mocking laugh.

"Aye, go on, pull the other leg, it's got bells on it."

"Aw, Ah didnae know ye had taken up Morris dancin, Erch...er...Special Constable McPherson," Fingers replied.

"Very smart, McGeachie," Erchie said, "But you ur under arrest for bein' in possession of petrol which Ah believe for to have been stolen. Also, whit dae ye know aboot two cases of Single Malt whisky that's been pinched frae the Glaiket Yob pub this night?"

"NUTHIN'!" Fingers said. Erchie suspected Fingers but couldn't prove it. He saw the arrest of Fingers McGeachie as another foot on the ladder of his ambition to join the regular City of Glasgow Police Force.

Erchie took Fingers by the arm and attempted to lead him away.

"Ye're makin' a big mistake, Erch...er...Special Constable McPherson," Fingers said. "If Ah was you ERCHIE, Ah would let me proceed wi' ma business or there is gonny be wan helluva stink."

"Is that so?" Erchie retorted, adding, "An' where dae ye think ye're goin' wi' this illicit cargo?"

"Ye don't want tae know, Erchie," Fingers said, ignoring Erchie's official title.

"Oh , but Ah dae," Erchie said. "Because no' only ur YOU in for it - HE'S in for it as well."

Ah am takin' the Fifth Amendment," Fingers said.

"We do nut hiv a Fifth Amendment," Erchie said knowingly. "You, McGeachie, hiv been seein' too many Humphrey Bogart pictures."

"Well, Ah'm keepin' ma trap shut so as no' tae implicate a very senior personage," Fingers said.

"There are NAE special personages as faur as me or the law is concerned," Erchie said stiffly. "Oot wi' it. Who is this petrol for?"

"A'right, ye really want tae know?" Fingers said, his mind racing.

"Indubitably!" Erchie said.

"Try and say that wi' a drink in ye" Fingers said.

"Less o' the levity," Erchie said. "The name? Who is this petrol for?"

Fingers whispered in Erchie's ear. The Special Constable staggered back stunned, his jaw drooping. "Ye...ye...ye don't really mean...?"

Fingers nodded and whistled softly as he looked to the sky.

"Ah canny believe it!" Erchie stammered, "CHIEF SUPER-INTENDENT...?"

"Oh, aye, him...but he's only gettin' hauf o' it. The other hauf's for Mr Sillitoe, the Chief Constable."

Erchie's jaw dropped even further. He saw his ambition flying out of the window should he take this situation any further. He dare not take Fingers in or all was lost.

"Bu...But, the Chief Superintendent is a born again Christian." Erchie stuttered.

"Well, if you don't keep yer mooth shut," Fingers said, "he'll be a born again convict. You say wan word o' this and they'll baith deny it and whose word is gonny be believed, eh? No' yours, A SPECIAL CONSTABLE, Erchie and yer chances o' gettin' intae the polis force wull be nil."

Fingers was correct, of course, and Erchie knew it. "A'right, Fingers, you win...THIS TIME. C'mon, Ah'll help ye push the barra up as faur as the coarner."

Erchie took hold of a shaft and Fingers, stepped back and allowed him to take the other shaft and walked behind him whistling as Erchie pushed on breathlessly until the arrived at the corner.

"Thanks, Special Constable," Fingers said, taking over the shafts.

As Fingers pushed on Erchie took hold of his arm. "Make sure they two know that AH know a' aboot this," he said. Fingers nodded. "Aye, ye're no' as daft as ye look, Spec. Erchie!" he said and went on his way...whistling merrily.

The next few days passed by without incident! The Luftwaffe were taking a holiday and the respite was welcomed by everybody.

Curdy McVey was overwhelmed by the petrol Fingers McGeachie had supplied and had cleared his stock. Ina was getting more excited as the days passed and Annie, accompanied by Rita, had visited Madame Ashe's and purchased for herself a neat two- piece suit in pink gabardine. Rasputin was happy back in camp and tinkering with bombs.

Wullie had a long lie and, scratching himself, emerged from his room and flopped down at the kitchen table.

"Aw, it was great tae have a long lie," he said to Annie, who poured him out a cup of sweet tea.

"True enough!" Annie said, "Ye just never know when ye're gonny get another good night's sleep withoot interruption."

"Ah had a funny dream," Wullie said, sipping the hot tea. "Ah dreamt that the Germans had invaded us. There was Paras ower the Barras and Ah was captured an' they slung me intae a room where they tortured me because of ma heroic exploits durin' the first war. Then tae make mattters worse, they broke intae the hoose here an' stole they two wally dugs."

Annie shook her head in despair.

"Ye'll need tae get they wally dugs aff yer mind, Wullie. Ye've got a wally dug fixation and there are mair important things in this world than wally dugs! Ah'm scunnered lookin' at them an' Ah'm gonny get shot o' them the first chance Ah get."

"They remind me o' ma maw," Wullie said, adding, "specially that wan," he added, nodding towards the pooch on the left hand side of the mantelpiece.

"Oh, Wullie, Ah despair o' you at times," Annie said, hiding a smile.

"Naw, ye know whit Ah mean, Annie," Wullie went on. "We grew up wi' them. They were always there in the hoose, ever since we were weans."

"Ye're gettin' nostalgic, Wullie," Annie said.

"Just in ma haun's," Wullie replied, flexing his hands, "but Ah'm takin' aspirin for it," he said.

Annie laughed.

"Aye, it's true," Wullie went on" As ye get aulder ye start tae reminisce." He sighed before going on. "Mind the time when we were weans and you used tae play beds in the street an' Ah used tae pull wee Greta Quinn's hair every chance Ah got?"

Annie nodded. "Oh, aye! She hated you for that"

"Quite right, tae!" Wullie laughed. "Ah wonder whit happened tae wee Baldy Quinn?"

"Ah think she merried a milkman," Annie said.

"They bloody milkmen are a' ower the place," Wullie said sourly.

Annie was not surprised at Wullie's outburst, only angry that he had allowed Ina McLatchie to slip through his fingers.

"Well, let's no' dwell on it," Annie said."We've got Ina's weddin' tae look forward tae, eh?"

Wullie did not reply. He sat staring ahead.

"Wullie, did ye no' hear me?" Annie said, raising her voice. "Ah'm sayin' it'll no' be long till Ina's weddin'."

WULLIE REMAINED SILENT.

"WULLIE!" Annie hollered.

"Er.. Aye, Ah heard ye," Wullie muttered emerging from his silence.

Annie put the boot in. "See, ye canny tell me that ye're no' kickin' yersel'. Ye loast yer chance and there's no' many o' us get a second chance o' happiness in this world!"

Wullie fell silent once more. What could he say? Could he admit to Annie that she was right all the time? That he DID have a deep affection for Ina McLatchie despite his constant sniping et her. Annie was rubbing it in.

"Ye should see the lovely outfit Ina got at Madame Ashe's," she said, "thanks tae Fingers."

"Aye, a'right," Wullie snapped.

"She'll be a lovely bride!" Annie went on.

"Aye, Ah said a'right, didn't Ah. Drap it."

Annie felt she had rubbed the salt in far enough and, placing an old blanket on top of the table, took the heavy, black iron from the top of the gas ring on the range, and began to iron Wullie's shirts.

A knock on the door had Annie replacing the flat iron back on top of the gas ring.

"Ah'll get it," she said.

Wullie heard muffled chat in the lobby and Annie entered with Ina at her heels.

"Ah'm just daein' a wee bit ironin', Ina," Annie said, retrieving the iron from the heat and proceeding with her chores.

"Aye, just go ahead," Ina said.

"Ah was just tellin' Wullie whit a lovely bride ye're gonny make," Annie said.

"Och, Annie," Ina blushed," a' brides are lovely...just like a' babies are lovely!"

Wullie looked up, "Ah've never seen a good lookin' wean yet." he said, "We look at them an' say they're lovely so as no' tae hurt their maw's feelin's. But maist o' them look like Churchill. Stick a cigar in their mooths an' ye couldnae tell the difference."

"Och, Wullie, you're too cynical," Annie reproved.

"Naw Ah'm no'," Wullie said huffily.

There was a short pause and Annie finished off the shirt she was ironing and, folding it, put it aside.

"No' be long noo, Ina, eh?" she said.

"Naw, a couple o' weeks," Ina said.

"It's just a shame yer da' wisnae here tae see it," Annie said.

"Oh, aye!" Ina said, her mind going to her father. "If he had have been here he would've stood up an' did his soliloquy frae Hamlet," she said with pride.

"Thank God he's no' here!" Wullie said.

"WULLIE!" Annie rebuked.

"He was the true professional," Ina said. "He would've loved tae have died wi' his make-up oan."

"Even his teeth in would've been an improvement," Wullie said.

Annie drew Wullie a 'look' and he shut up.

"Ah'm sure ma da' WULL be at the weddin'," Ina said.

"Well, if he could pop doon...or up...for tae see ye there's nae reason he canny attend yer weddin'," Wullie said.

"There's wan thing Ah'll say aboot ma da'," Ina went on, "he wisnae afraid o' dyin'."

"That's because he died manys a time oan the stage," Wullie said dryly.

"Ma da' was a great actor," Ina blurted. "He wance played a Redskin."

"Geronimo?" Wullie asked, raising his brows.

"Naw, The Attack of the killer Tomatoes. He was the leadin' tomato." Ina said.

"That figures!" Wullie commented. "So, how can ye say yer auld man's a great actor when he's cast as a tomato?"

"Work's work, Wullie," Ina said, ignoring his sneers.

"Ah would imagine that playin' a vegetable would be Auld

Jake's forte," Wullie said. "He's was never oot that lavvy! He would've got an Oscar if he'd played a leak!"

"Say whit ye like," Ina said, "But he had a big followin'."

"Aye, a' dugs followin' the smell," Wullie said cattily.

"Ye've nae right tae say that, Wullie," Ina said angrily, "Ma da' had an affinity wi' dugs efter his work wi' Rin-Tin-Tin and when dugs followed him in the street they were really followin' Rin-Tin-Tin, a big star. Just like you would follow Betty Greble or Ah would follow Errol Flynn."

"That means nothin'," Wullie said. "You would follow Quasimodo!"

"Ah don't have tae noo, dae Ah?" Ina said.

"He'd be an improvement oan Charlie Gallagher," Wullie said. "And he's used tae ringin' bells...doorbells. They've got that in common."

Wullie wasn't proud of himself. He had sworn to himself that he would stop being snidey to Ina. But he had been at it so long that it all came automatically and without thinking to him. He had not missed Annie's glare throughout his banter with Ina.

"Ah just came in tae see ye, Annie," Ina said, "and tae ask ye if we should maybe have a hen night?"

"Well, Ah don't mind," Annie said, "jist as long as you don't mind gettin' paraded up an' doon the street wi' a veil ower yer heid and a chanty full o' confetti in yer haun'!"

"Oh, Ah never thought o' that," Ina cried. "Ah thought that auld custom had died oot?"

"No' a bit of it!" Annie said. "It's right good fun if ye can let yersel' get intae the spirit o' things. Ah remember when Sammy and me were gettin' merried," Annie said, her mind going back. "Ah was workin' in Templeton's Carpet Factory and the lassies dressed me up in' a white veil and stuck a chanty full o' salt in ma haun's. Then they paraded me through the streets shoutin' 'Hard Up!', Hard Up!' sherekin me and folk laughed an' threw money intae the potty."

"Aw, Ah don't think Ah could dae that, Annie?" Ina said. "Ah'd be too embarrassed, so Ah would."

"Ye'll need tae get used tae chantys efter yer merried," Wullie said.

Ina blushed again. "Ma da' wull be lookin' doon at me this minute," she said, steering the conversation away.

"Or UP?" Wullie said.

"Naw, Ah'm sure he's in heaven," Ina sighed. "Him an' Rin-Tin-Tin and a' they big stars. And, don't forget, stars look doon, Wullie, no' Up."

The next two weeks flew in. The Calton Social Club had been booked for the reception Curdy McVey, now with a full quota of fuel, had generously offered his hearse to transport the bride to St Alphonsus' Church, in London Road. Ina thanked him for his generous offer and accepted it on condition it did not contain a corpse — as his hearse did at Rita's wedding where Rita, Wullie and Curdy sat in the front and the corpse of a Mrs McGinty lay in the back. Curdy assured her that only live people would be transported.

Annie was pleased with her own outfit and Charlie had proudly told them that a guard of honour would be there, standing to attention outside the church and making an arch with milk ladles. Fingers McGeachie had managed to acquire a 120 spool for Curdy's Brownie camera. Film spools were like gold and hard to acquire and Curdy could only shake his head in admiration of Fingers. He wondered where the smooth Mr McGeachie had acquired the precious film and had not noticed the W.D. stamp on it. Or, if he did, he was not acquainted with the War Department's trademark.

It was now the eve of the wedding and Ina, dressed in her wedding outfit knocked coyly at Annie's door.

Annie brought her in and made her stand in the middle of the room.

"Whit dae ye think?, Annie?" Ina said, doing a full twirl.

"Aw, ye're lovely, hen!" Annie said, dabbing her eyes at the same time.

"Ah'm a' excited!" Ina said, adding, "Ah only wish ma da' was here!" and she, too, began dabbing her eyes.

Wullie had been down to St Alphonsus' to make sure everything was as it should be.

Father Casey would officiate at the Nuptial Mass and the bouquet and buttonholes had arrived at 27 Well Street from Mary Fox's shop.

Earlier, Annie, Ina and Rita kept their appointment with Madame Wee Nellie where Annie and Ina had a 'perm' and Rita had a Marcel Wave.

The Calton Social Club had been scrubbed clean and smelled of disinfectant and The Bachles Band had been booked. Curdy McVey collected his best 'funeral' suit from Pullar's the Cleaners and Wullie was delighted that his blue serge suit, worn only on very special occasions, still fitted him. He had made sure he had a pocketful of coins for 'The Scramble' when half the children in the street would be waiting at the close-mouth to see the bride emerge and, as the bridal car moved off, there would be a mad scramble to retrieve the money Wullie would toss out of the car window. Some of the more astute children would note the date so as to be on the alert nine months later when the Christening would take place and the Godmother, on the way to church carrying the new baby would also be carrying two abernethy biscuits with a half-crown jammed between them as was the custom. This would be handed to the first child to be seen.

After leaving St Alphonsus' Church, situated in London Road, near Kent Street where 'The Barras' began and from where they spread out, Wullie was stopped by Wee Frankie Johnston, one of the stallholders.

"Wullie!" Frankie cried, taking him by the arm.

"Whit is it?" Wullie grumped, a bit annoyed.

"Here," Frankie said, pushing a brown paper parcel into his hands. "That's for Ina, a wee Weddin' present frae some o' the Barra Boys."

Wullie was touched by the generous thought.

"Ah'm sure she'll be pleased!" Wullie said.

"It's a pair o' caun'le sticks...real brass," Frankie said proudly, adding, "Noo, if there's anythin' she needs just gie us a shout, a'right wee man?"

Before Wullie could answer he reeled at the heavy slap on the back and Wee Frankie was gone.

Wullie watched him disappear in amongst the stalls. Frankie may be wee, he thought, but, like many of his colleagues, he had a big heart.

Wullie arrived home with the candkesticks under his arm

and , walking in, was taken aback at the sight of Ina McLatchie. He had never seen her look so lovely! Aye, Charlie Gallagher was a lucky man, he thought, and HE was a fool. Ina was delighted with the candlesticks and said she would make sure Frankie and his pals would get a slice of wedding cake.

"Ina's beautiful, Wullie, int she?" Annie enthused.

Annie was rubbing it in, Wullie thought. But he had to agree. He nodded. "Aye, she is...very!" he said softly

A loud knock on the door made Annie jump. "Who could that be?" she said, hurrying to the door.

Wullie and Ina heard muffled voices coming from the lobby and Annie came hurrying in.

"Quick," she said to Ina, "put that on." She threw a house-coat and Ina hurriedly put it, wondering...

"Right," Annie said, "ye can come in noo," she called out.

Charlie Gallagher walked slowly in, his head bowed.

"Ye should know it's bad luck for to see the bride in her wedding gown before the ceremony," Annie said reprovingly.

When Charlie entered, Wullie immediately poured him a large glass of V.P. Handing it to him he could not help but notice Charlie's shaking hand.

"Boy, have you got the nerves, Charlie!" Wullie said, smiling.

Charlie took the glass, almost spilling the contents.

"Ah'd like a word wi' Ina if youse don't mind...alone!"

Annie and Ina exchanged glances.

"Ye can say whatever it is in front o' Annie and Wullie," Ina said, narrowing her eyes.

Charlie stared down at the linoleum and shuffled his feet.

He gave a nervous cough and, without looking up, almost whispered, "Ah'm sorry, Ina, Ah canny mairry ye."

Ina let out a scream and flopped on to the chair, her hand coming up to her mouth to stifle her distress. Wullie immediately darted forward and snatched the drink from Charlie's hand, spilling most of it. And, turning he retrieved the bottle from the table, placed it in the sideboard cupboard and slammed the door.

Annie lifted a cushion and bashed Charlie over the head.

"Swine!" she said angrily. She put an comforting arm around Ina's shoulder which was heaving to her heavy sobs.

"PIG!", Wullie snarled.

"Oh, don't mention PIG, Wullie," Annie said, "it reminds me o' weddin's past." Then, turning her rage on Charlie, she snapped:

"Right you, whit brought this oan?"

Charlie sank back in the chair as though retreating from an impending attack.

"Ah jist realised that Ah love another and it widnae be fair tae you, Ina, for me tae take ye as ma bride when ma heart is somewhere else, so it widnae!" Charlie said, avoiding Annie's glare.

"Ye just fun' this oot the day before yer weddin'?" Annie snapped, belting him once more with the cushion.

Charlie raised his arm, shielding himself from the pounding.

"Ah'm really sorry but Ah feel it widnae be right for tae mairry you, Ina, if Ah couldnae devote ma whole heart tae ye. It widnae be fair!" Charlie said.

"FAIR?" Annie hollered, "FAIR, whit a cheek you've got. Whit's fair aboot jiltin' a lassie on the eve of her weddin'? Who is this new love o' yours anyway?"

Charlie shuffled uneasily on the chair.

"It's Daisy," he said.

"Who the Hell's Daisy?" Wullie demanded.

"Ma hoarse," Charlie said quietly.

"YOU ur gien' up this lovely lassie for a HOARSE?" Annie cried.

"We've been together for a long time," Charlie said apologetically, "When Ah telt Daisy Ah was gettin' married Ah could see right away that she was dead jealous."

"She telt ye that, did she?" Wullie said mockingly.

"Naw, but she's been goin' aboot wi' a long face," Charlie said.

"A LONG FACE?" Wullie cried. "Charlie — EVERY hoarse has a long face. It's the wey they're built.." Wullie made a gesture with his hand mockingly , elongating his face.

"And she kicked me an a'!" Charlie said.

"On the heid, Ah think!" Annie said.

"She used tae eat oot ma haun'," Charlie said, "Noo she eats ma haun'.

Ina stood up and, with effort, pulled the engagement from her finger and threw it at Charlie.

"Here," she cried, "see if that fits yer hoarses hoof." Saying that she flopped into the chair once more and, cradling her head in her arms on the table top, she burst into uncontrollable sobbing. Seeing Ina's distress only fired Annie's anger all the more.

"You've a right cheek on ye," she snapped. "But Ina's lucky tae have fun' oot how spineless ye are before mairryin' ye. Ah hope a' yer mulk curdles!"

"You don't know the relationship a man can hiv wi' his hoarse," Charlie protested. Putting his hand on his heart, he stood erect and and solemnly quoted.

"A four-legged friend, A four-legged friend, She'll never let you down, She's honest and faithful right up to the end, that one, two, three, one, two, three, four-legged friend." And then he sat down.

"He's been bloody influenced by Roy Rogers!" Wullie said, throwing up his arms.

"He's Roger the Dodger, that's for sure," Annie commented.

Charlie approached Ina and, hesitating for a moment, said, "Ah hope ye can find it in yer heart for tae forgive me, Ina."

Ina looked up at his face and howled louder.

Charlie headed for the door and left...but not before a cushion smashed into the back of his head.

Wullie, too, felt like strangling Charlie but, at the same time, he wanted to shake his hand. Annie had said that you don't get two chances for happiness in this world! That you had to grab it as it came along.

Annie was sitting consoling Ina who was still sobbing bitterly. "Jilted!" she said through her tears. "How am Ah ever gonny live it doon?"

"It's best it happened noo, Ina." Annie said softly.

"Ye're right," Wullie said, "Before ye knew it there would be you, Charlie and the hoarse a' in the same bed."

That brought a fleeting smile to Ina's face.

"But what am Ah gonny dae aboot a' the guests who'll be turnin' up for the weddin'?" Ina sobbed.

"Well, hen, there's no' much ye can dae at this late stage, is there?" Annie said, squeezing her arm.

"It's better jist tae let things go ahead as if there was a weddin'. Wullie'll look efter things, won't ye Wullie?"

Wullie had no hesitation. "Aye," he said, "Jist leave everything tae me."

Ina rose and kissed his cheek.

"Ye're a pal, Wullie!" she said

Wullie flushed and stammered, "Don't worry aboot anythin', Ina."

Wullie left the house and Annie put the kettle on.

"We'll have a wee cuppa tea, Ina," she said. "A wee cuppa tea works wonders."

Ina gave a weak smile. Annie made the tea and poured two cups. Sitting down beside Ina at the table, she took her hand and squeezed it affectionately.

"Tell me truthfully, Ina. Did ye love him?"

Without hesitation, Ina said, "Ah liked him, Annie."

"It's no' the same, hen," Annie said softly.

"Time's goin' on, Annie," Ina choked.

"Aye, and ye shouldnae waste it, hen," Annie said. "Ye must remember that you've still got a lot o' life still tae live - the Luftwaffe permittin'..."

Ina smiled at the inference.

"Ye don't want tae be lumbered wi' a bloke who, efter a few months o' marriage suddenly discovers he loves his hoarse mair than you."

"We could've made a go of it," Ina said quietly.

"Naw, hen," Annie said. "This is probably a blessin' in disguise."

"But whit aboot a' they people? A' ma freen's, that'll be turnin' up at the chapel the morra expectin' see take part in a weddin' ceremony?"

"So, they'll get tae a party instead. They'll no' complain," Annie said.

"But it's the stigma!" Ina said, dabbing a tear once more.

"Ina, hen, you're no' the only lassie that's ever been jilted," Annie consoled. "And there's a lot o' it goin' aboot the noo. A' these lassies runnin' efter the Yanks and it's the Yanks that end up runnin'. Ah'm tellin' ye this is the year of the jilted bride, so don't you dwell oan it. If anythin' Charlie did ye a favour.

Ah'm jist mad that he left it tae the last minute."

"Ye're a tower o' strength, Annie," Ina said, kissing Annie's cheek.

Annie laughed, "There's plenty fish in the sea, Ina...and Ah know wan that's jist ripe for hookin'."

Annie thought of all the candles she had lit down at St Alphonsus' and her pleadings that Wullie and Ina walk down that terrazzo aisle and "tie-the-knot".

Charlie did HER a favour.

Yes, she reckoned, prayers DO work!

Wullie had made his way down to the Calton Social Club and was now in deep conversation with Big Alex, the hall caretaker.

"And that's whit happened, Alex!" Wullie was saying.

Big Alex's lips tightened.

"Charlie, eh?" he said through his teeth. "Think Ah should get the boys oan tae him?"

Wullie shook his head.

"Naw, naw!" he said, "Folk need their mulk. Besides, it's maybe the best thing tha happened. The point noo is that we want the reception for tae go ahead as planned. There's nae wey we can contact a' the people by the morra for to tell them this goo...er...terrible news. Ah mean they're scattered frae a' ower the place...Brigton, Soo Side, Possil and Newton Mearns, although Ah don't know how SHE got in there. Wull that be a'right then, Alex?"

"Aye, don't worry, Wullie," Alex said. "Gie Ina a kiss frae me."

Wullie laughed, "Naw, naw, she might get ideas."

Wullie left the smell of disinfectant behind and hurried along Stevenston Street to St Alphonsus' Chapel House.

Father Casey was very sympathetic and suggested he visit Ina to bring her some solace.

"Naw, naw," Wullie said, "Annie and me are takin' care o' that, Father. You're a busy man!"

But Father Casey, being the reverend gentleman that he was, was up at the house and sitting by Ina's side within the hour.

"Just think on this way, my child," he said. "It is HIS will," Father Casey pointed a forefinger upwards.

"Auld Shug frae up the stairs?" Ina said, her mouth dropping open.

"No, no, HIM," Father Casey emphasised, "your Father in heaven."

"How dae ye know her Faither's IN heaven?" Wullie said. "He was an auld reprobate."

"He was nut!" Ina snapped.

"I'm referring to your heavenly Father," Father Casey said, hiding his impatience. "Dear GOD!"

"That's whit Ah said when Charlie Gallagher came oot wi' that horrendous news...that betrayal!" Annie said.

Ina sobbed, "Father," she said, "It's bad enough gettin' jilted for another wumman...but a HOARSE!"

"It's no' even street trained," Wullie said. "It craps a' ower the place."

Father Casey hid a smile, put his hand on Ina's head and said a prayer. Before leaving, he turned at the door and said, "Now remember. It is HIS will, so don't be angry and do anything foolish...like becoming a Protestant or something."

Next morning Wullie stood on the steps of St Alphonsus' and greeted the guests as they arrived. After explaining things he directed them to The Calton Social Cub, just a few hundred yards away. And it was there, after a drum roll from The Bachles, that he called the gathering to order.

"Ladies and Gentlemen," he began, "Ah know that youse have all come here for to celebrate weddin' of Ina McLatchie and Charlie Gallagher and that youse now know that the weddin' wull not take place. Wullie paused to gather his breath. "Youse may not know, however, the reason that this calamity has happened," he went on. "The reason that poor Ina has been jilted by said Charlie Gallagher is that he falled in love wi' his hoarse. Noo, anybody that would gie up the lovely, if no' a bit overweight, Ina McLatchie for a hoarse, can nut be the full shullin'. Ah admit that Charlie Gallagher did nut use the expression that he felled in love wi' his hoarse, but that he loved his hoarse which was noo goin' aboot wi' a long face. Well, Ah ask ye? Who wants a shoart face hoarse? Anywey, The Bachles ur here for your pleasure and seein' the hall has been Lysolised, it would be a shame for no' tae use

111

these attributics while we have gote them. So, enjoy yersel's yer in yer aunty's. All weddin presents that hivnae been pawned wull be returned, in due course."

A round of applause ended Wullie's narrative and Ina kissed his cheek and thanked him.

The Bachles struck up a St Bernard's Waltz and Annie grabbed her brother and pulled him on to the floor.

"Ye know whit this means, Wullie, don' ye?" she said as they danced.

"Whit does whit mean?" Wullie grunted.

"Ina' a free wumman again. Ah keep tellin' ye, ye don't usually get two chances for happiness in this world."

"Whit's that got tae dae wi' me?" Wullie said, knitting his brows.

"Don't let this opportunity go by, Wullie," Annie begged.

Wullie missed a step. "Oops!" he said. "Ye've got me Ah don't know whit Ah'm daein'," he said shyly.

"She didnae love Charlie, y'know." Annie said.

"Let me think aboot it," Wullie said. "Ah don't know if Ah'm ready tae settle doon."

"Ur ye waitin' till yer ninety or somethin'?" Annie snapped, getting impatient. "Let her be able tae run her fingers through yer hair while ye've still got it."

"Very funny!" Wullie said, making a face.

"Well, the lassie's been through a terrible trauma," Annie said sympathetically, "at least gie her a wee day oot to lift her mind. Take her tae the pictures or somethin'. Wull ye dae that, Wullie? No' jist for Ina, but for me, eh?"

Wullie hesitated, "Aye, a'right, Annie...for you, hen."

Fingers McGeachie hurriedly left the corner of the hall where he was trapped by half-a-dozen pretty girls. Pulling Wullie aside he demanded to know if what Wullie had said was true and when Wullie confirmed every word of his address was true fact the steam blew from Fingers' ears. This was not on! He immediately swore to "dub up, no' only Charlie, but his hoarse as well!"

Wullie talked him out of such drastic action and only hoped that Charlie and Fingers didn't run to each other in the near future. Not, at least, until Fingers' anger had abated.

The Bachles struck up the last waltz and Ina grabbed Wullie and pulled him on to the floor.

"How ur ye feelin', hen?" Wullie quietly asked.

"Life goes oan," Ina said philosophically.

"Would ye...er...would ye like for tae go tae the pictures the morra...wi' me?" Wullie asked shyly.

"Oh, aye, of coorse Ah would, Wullie, thank ye," Ina bubbled.

Everybody enjoyed the night and all the sympathies were heaped upon Ina who discovered that she was more hurt by Charlie reneging than by losing him.

She went to bed that night exhausted but not too unhappy. She closed her eyes, hoping she would get a full night's sleep with no interference from the Luftwaffe.

For tomorrow was another day...a busy one!

Six

There were no raids that night and, fully refreshed, Ina prepared for her big date with Wullie McSorley. She was extra attentive when applying her make-up and chose her favourite dress and with her new hat, recently acquired from Margaret Forrester's, she knocked on Annie's door.

Annie's face lit up. "Come in, Ina, ye're lookin' lovely. Wullie'll no' be a minute!" she said.

Wullie, hearing voices, stepped into the room. He had brought his blue serge suit out of hibernation and was going to wear it.

"My, ye're lookin' smart, Wullie!" Ina said.

"Aye, well...er...c'mon, let's go," Wullie said.

Wullie and Ina emerged from the closemouth arm-in-arm and walked up the street on and to London Road, where they crossed and stood at the tram stop outside Ramage's grocery store. A green, number eighteen car, going to Springburn, was along within minutes.

They sat upstairs, in the cabin above the driver and headed for town where they got off in Argyle Street. Wullie and Ina went into Lewis' Polytechnic, "The Polly" and enjoyed browsing through every floor.

They then crossed the street and entered Woolworths where Ina purchased a lipstick and a bottle of leg tan. Embarrassed, Wullie moved over to the stand holding Ready Made Reading Glasses, two shillings and sixpence a pair. Or, in Wullie's parlance, "hauf-a-croon". Then next door and into Marks and Spencers. "No, sorry," the girl assistant said, "no silk stockings!"

Wullie and Ina walked along Argyle Street towards 'The Heilin' Man's Umbrella" the affectionate title given to the railway bridge that ran across the street between Union Street and

114

Hope Street. But before arriving there, they turned up Union Street which joined Renfield Street. Crossing Gordon Street, the couple turned into Drury Street and Wullie escorted Ina into The Horseshoe Bar where, sitting in corner, Wullie sipped a pint of McEwan's beer and Ina, a sweet sherry.

They sat and chatted, and chatted about everything, everything but Charlie or his horse and Wullie found himself very comfortable in Ina's company. For of all the years they knew each other, this was the first time they had ever been alone together.

There was a small queue outside the Paramount Cinema, in Renfield Street, which was showing Casablanca, with Humphrey Bogart and Ingrid Bergman. Ina cried at the end and they left the hall in daylight. Wullie suggested a cup of tea at Miss Cranston' Tearoom and they were lucky to get a table. Later they walked along to George Square where there was a "Wings for Victory" display with a real British bomber standing there.

"Would ye look at that! Wullie said proudly. "We'll show them. We'll gie them a touch o' their ain medicine, Aye!"

Neither of them felt like going home and decided to take their time. They crossed down Mitchell Street and on to Trongate, through Glasgow Cross and on up London Road, past Charlottle Street on to Glasgow Green.

The Army Catering Corp were giving a display here and a field kitchen had be set up where the soldiers showed off their culinary skills. Also there was a display of Barrage Balloons, five of them, tethered to the ground and gazed on with awe by the onlookers.

"Ye widnae think they were so big, widn't ye no'?" Ina said. For, from the ground, the balloons were mere dots in the sky.

Wullie nodded. "Aye, right enough!" he said. "And it's good tae see oor servicemen are gettin' well fed," he added.

"Well, ye know the auld sayin', Wullie," Ina said. "An army goes tae war on its stomach!"

Wullie and Ina called in at Peter Rossi's for a McCallum before heading down Well Street.

Ina stopped at her door.

"Thanks for a lovely day, Wullie," she said, smiling.

"Ma pleasure, Ina!" Wullie said, slightly embarrassed. "Would ye like tae come in for a wee dram?" Ina said. "Ah believe there's some left. Ma da' always liked a wee nightcap."

Wullie nodded and entered the spotlessly clean, neat house.

"Sit ye doon oan the settee, Wullie," Ina said, indicating the rexine couch. Wullie sat at the edge, a little nervously.

Ina poured Wullie a large Scotch and a sweet sherry for herself and sat on the couch beside him.

They clinked glasses. "Good health, Wullie!" Ina smiled.

"Here's lookin' at you, kid," Wullie lisped.

Ina laughed and Wullie winked.

They sat listening to the wireless for the next few hours. They laughed with Tommy Handley in "I.T.M.A." and enjoyed Wilfred Pickles in "Have A Go!" and Vera Lynn, "The Forces Sweetheart" in sentimental mood. Geraldo and his Orchestra played the latest from America.

Ina lay in bed that night, her mind racing through everything that had happened that day. She couldn't believe that she had spent the entire day with Wullie McSorley and was not the butt of his sarcasm. She closed her eyes. Yes, she liked this Wullie McSorley much better.

"Here's lookin' at you, kid!" She laughed at the thought of it and drifted into slumber...a much happier person than she was the day previously.

Wullie staggered into the kitchen after a good, uninterrupted night's sleep. Annie already had the tea in the pot and under its cosy on top of the table. Wullie washed his hands under the cold tap and sat down while Annie poured out the tea and pushed over a plate with hot toast.

Annie poured out her own tea and sat down at the table. They sat in silence and Annie was getting more and more agitated.

"Well?" she said finally, unable to hide her curiosity any longer.

"Well whit?" Wullie said, looking up.

"How did it go?"

"How did whit go?" Wullie asked.

Exasperated, Annie stood her full height, put her hands on her waist and snapped, "Yer date wi' Ina?"

Wullie shrugged, "Aye, no' bad!" he said.

"Jist 'no' bad?" Annie said.

"Aye, well, good," Wullie said.

"Ah dinae hear ye comin' in," Annie said. "Ah went tae bed early. So, it was good, eh?"

"That's whit Ah said," Wullie said irritably.

"Where di youse go?" Annie demanded.

Wullie gave Annie their full itinerary and a run down on the chat and this satisfied her. She reckoned that she could expect no more. Well, not for a first date anyway!

The door flew open and a radiant Ina stormed in.

"Oh, Annie!" she said. "Ah feel like a big load has been lifted aff me. It's amazin' whit a difference a day makes, intit?"

"Aye, ye're right, Ina, hen." Annie agreed. "'C'mon, sit ye doon an' have a wee cuppa tea."

Ina sat at the table and Annie poured. "Mornin', Wullie," Ina cooed.

"Aye, 'mornin'," Wullie said gruffly.

"Don't mind him, Ina, "Annie said, scowling at Wullie, "he's always crochity in the mornin'."

Ina laughed. "Ye know somethin' else, Annie," she bubbled, "Ah'm suddenly no' a bit angry wi' Charlie. It's been the best thing, Ah think!"

"Aye, well better findin' oot noo than later," Annie said wisely.

"Aye, true enough! " Ina agreed.

"Did ye get an extra pinta on yer doorstep this mornin' Ina?" Annie asked with a chuckle.

"Naw," Ina said with a laugh. "Ah'm surprised Ah got any mulk at a'!"

"He left me an extra pinta," Annie said. "Tryin' tae sook in but he's not on."

"Ach, Annie, forget a' aboot it. Ah'm sure him an' his hoarse wull be very happy," Ina said.

Wullie rose from the table. "Ye...er...fancy a wee walk, Ina?" he found himself saying.

"Naw, sorry Wullie," Ina said. "It's ma turn o' the stairs."

Each household up the close had to take their turns in washing the stone stairs and it was chore that nobody enjoyed...except Annie who laid into them with gusto. Everybody knew when Annie had scrubbed the stairs. She was not sparing with the pipe clay and the stair sides gleamed white.

"Och, away ye go, Ina," Annie said. "Ah'll dae the stairs for ye!"

"You wull not!" Ina said. "You've enough tae dae. Maybe some other time, Wullie, but thanks for the invitation."

Wullie grunted and left the room. He didn't expect Ina McLatchie to turn him down at all...and especially for the stairs.

Wullie walked up to Mr Adams' shop and bought his morning Bulletin and strolled across to Monteith Row and, as it was a bright day and not too cold, he ambled down to the Glasgow Green. For a while he stood watching two pensioners playing draughts on a giant size tiled board on the ground. The old men used a hook on a pole and sat there, staring at the board and watching all the moves with the tenseness of a Grand Masters Chess contest.

Wullie left the two men and their audience to get on with it and ambled on down to the Clydeside, Leaning on a fence he watched Ben Parsonage, of the Glasgow Humane Society, rowing out into the river. He wondered if Mr Parsonage was searching for another drowning victim or merely rowing about for some exercise?

He decided not to wait to find out. Finding an unoccupied bench, near the river, he sat down to read his paper.

The war news was good!

He sat on reading the paper from cover-to-cover, stopping only to get up and buy a "poke" from an ice-cream vendor who came past on his bicycle.

It was almost lunch time when Wullie headed home. Mr Parsonage was still out in the river and Wullie wondered if he was looking once more for an suicide victim?

He would never know for he walked on without looking back. The old men were still hovering over their draughts board with all the intensity of generals planning a battle. Wullie stopped for a moment and continued on.

Crossing London Road he heard the clanging of a tram's bell. Looking up he saw Rita giving him a cheery wave from the platform. He waved back and carried on down Well Street.

Wullie noted immediately that the stairs had been done. The strong smell of the Lysol disinfectant hit him as soon as he walked in the close. Ina was down on her knees just putting the finishing touches to her door step when he arrived at Annie's door, Ina looked up and leaned back on her heels and, wiping her brow, said, "Ah, ye're back, Wullie. It's a nice day!"

"Aye!" Wullie agreed, putting his key in the door...although it was as usual, unlocked.

"There's.. er.. still a wee dram left in that boattle, Wullie, if ye'd...er...care tae...?"

"Er...aye, aye," Wullie stammered.

"Right then," Ina said, standing up. "Jist gie me five minutes to tidy masel' up a bit and come in."

"Aye, right!" Wullie said.

Annie was drying dishes when he entered. "Had a good walk, then?" she said, looking over her shoulder.

"Aye, went doon the Green," Wullie said.

"Want somethin' tae eat?" Annie said.

"Er.. naw, naw, no' the noo, Annie," Wullie said. "Er.. Ina's asked me in for a wee dram."

"Oh, aye?" Annie said, raising her eyebrows.

"So, Ah'll.. er.. jist be .. er.. goin' in the noo," Wullie stuttered.

Ina , wearing a brand new, gaily-coloured, 'peeny' opened the door and, smiling, invited Wullie in.

She indicated the settee and Wullie sat down and Ina handed him a good glass of whisky. She poured herself a sweet sherry and joined him on the couch.

"Here's lookin' at you, kid," she laughed, raising her glass.

They sat and talked...and talked. Ina told how much she missed her father, of how frightened she was of the air raids and of how good a neighbour Annie was. Her hand accidentally touched Wullie's who drew his hand quickly away. He stood up in confusion.

"Ah'd...er...better be gettin' in," he said.

"It's early yet," Ina said.

"Na, naw, Ah'll get in. Thanks for the dram," he stammered and was gone. Ina wondered what she had said or done to offend him?

"You're in early!" Annie said.

"Aye, well...er..." Wullie began.

"Aye, well...er...nothin'," Annie said. "It's aboot time you knew whit ye're daein'!"

Wullie wondered what he had done to earn this rebuke?

Annie went out on to the landing and, knocking Ina's door, invited her in for a "wee cuppa tea".

Ina followed Annie in and, sitting at the table, thanked her for the invitation.

"The time's no' right yet for you ta be sittin' in there alone," Annie said, pouring the tea.

"Ye're very thoughtful, Annie, " Ina said. "Ye've been like a sister tae me."

Annie felt a lump come in her throat and swallowed. She looked at Wullie and nodded towards Ina. Wullie knew what she was on about. Annie in her unsubtle way, was urging Wullie to pop the question. He ignored her.

Passing him by to put the teapot on the gas ring, she kicked his ankles. Wullie let out a howl and rubbed his foot.

"Whit's up, Wullie?" Ina said.

"Ah've got Annieitis oan ma fit!" he growled. Annie ignored him.

"Have ye heard any mair aboot Sammy, Annie?" Ina asked with concern

Annie shook her head. "Naw, no' a cheep!" she said. "Ah worry a' the time."

"Dae ye think he'll try tae escape?" Ina said.

"Knowin' Sammy Ah widnae put it past him. He's always been wan for takin' a chance," she said and glowring at Wullie, added. "Ye've got tae take chances in this world. Ye don't get second chances so ye don't. Right, Wullie?"

Their eyes met, Wullie's narrowing but he could not mistake Annie's nod of the head towards Ina.

Annie was firing on all cylinders. Wullie ignored her.

"True enough!" Ina said, "Ye've got tae take chances in this world or ye get naewhere. Steve Brodie took a chance."

"Who's Steve Brodie?" Annie asked quizically.

"He took a chance and went ower Niagra Falls in a barrel." Ina said knowingly.

"An' whit happened?" Annie asked.

"Ah think he got killed," Ina said, "but Ah'm no' sure. The point is he DID take the chance and he is doon in history noo."

"Aye, and he's doon onder six feet o' grun' as well, "Wullie sniped. "That's whit HE got for takin' a chance."

Annie glared at him.

"WULLIE, will ye gie yersel' a shake," she yelled.

"Whit's up, Annie?" Ina asked. "Whit is it? Is it yer ankle, Wullie?"

"Naw, it's his spine," Annie said contemptuously. "He hisnae got wan."

"Naw, naw, Ah don't believe that," Ina said in Wullie's defence.

Wullie's mind was racing. Annie was trying to be a matchmaker, he knew that. He knew, too, that when the war was over and Sammy repatriated and back home and Rita and Rasputin taking up residence, things would be getting pretty crowded. But not crowded enough that he should consider matrimony for the sake of space.

But he was very fond of Ina although he had never shown it. In fact he had deliberately been rude to her in case he should have allowed his real feelings to show. But Annie had always known there was a spark in Wullie's heart. She must have seen something in him that should not have shown. He did like Ina.. very much! Love was not a word that Wullie or his peers used much. That was for the Hollywood films. "Fond" was a less embarrassing, gooey word. And Wullie was FOND of Ina. His defences were down and he regretted every rude and facetious phrase he had ever used to her. He was suddenly brave and wondered if Ina had spiked his drink? Of course she hadn't, that was just his cynical mind working again, he decided.

Annie, sipping her tea, watched curiously as Wullie suddenly rose and approached Ina.

"Ina," he said quietly.

"Aye, Wullie?" Ina looked up curiously.

"Ah was jist thinkin'," Wullie went on. "That...er...two-piece suit outfit ye bought for the weddin'...?"

"Aye, Wullie?"

"It's a shame it's tae go tae waste," Wullie said.

"Ah'll survive," Ina said.

Wullie took a deep breath and stood his full height.

"Look, Ina," he said, "Ah know Ah've gied ye a loat o' stick ower the years. Ah...Ah'm sorry!"

Annie spluttered on her tea and narrowed her eyes, wondering what was coming next.

Ina blushed slightly.

"Oh, Wullie," she said, "Ah don't know ye like this! Are ye tryin' tae say somethin'?"

Wullie gave a slight embarrassing cough.

"Ina," he said nervously, "Ah...er...Ah would be honoured if you would be ma wife!"

Annie jumped from her chair and, swiping the wally dugs from the mantelshelf, thrust them into Ina's arms.

"Congratulations!!" she whooped. "Here's yer first weddin' present."

Ina smiled, "Ah hivnae said 'yes'," she said.

Wullie's face fell. Perhaps he had taken Ina too much for granted. He turned and walked sadly away.

"Wullie," Ina said softly.

Wullie turned. Ina stood, her arms outstretched. Wullie smiled broadly and hurried over to a welcome and warm embrace.

"Ah'll try tae make ye happy, hen," he whispered.

Annie did a jig, took the V.P. from the sideboard cupboard, replaced it and produced a bottle of single Malt whisky.

She poured three glasses and after a lot of hugging and kissing, they toasted the future.

Annie hugged Ina and kissed Wullie.

"Ah thought ye'd never get around tae that!" Annie said.

"Ah was pickin' ma ain time," Wullie replied with a mischievous twinkle.

"Whit aboot a' the arrangements?" Annie said with concern

"Ah'll attend tae everythin'," Wullie said and Ina gazed lovingly into his eyes. Her 'man' could do ANYTHING, she reckoned.

"Ah'll go doon and see big Alex and arrange for the hall for to be available," Wullie said.

"But when is the big day?" Annie asked.

"Ah'd like tae know that tae," Ina said.

"How aboot in three weeks time, eh?" Wullie said. "Ah'll get Father Casey tae read the banns and arrange everythin'."

"Whit aboot the caterin'?" Annie said. "Ina used up a' her coupons on her weddin' that never happened."

"Ah'll have a word wi' Fingers," Wullie said.

"They should make Fingers the Prime Minister," Annie said. "He never lets ye doon."

"Aye, well Ah'm sure he'll come through as always," Wullie said, "even if it's jist a wee roastin' pig, eh?"

Annie and Ina burst out laughing.

"And Ah'm sure The Bachles wull turn up again," Wullie said. Then with a sigh, he added, "Aye, everythin's perfect!"

Annie went suddenly quiet. "No' everythin', Wullie," she said softly.

"Whit's missin'?" Wullie said.

"Sammy's missin', that's who's missin'."

Annie's eyes filled up. Wullie put an arm around her shoulder. "Don't worry, hen," he said softly. "Ah'm sure everythin' wull work oot just fine."

Wullie left Annie and Ina sipping tea and gossiping. He went straight down to St Alphonsus' Chapel House and saw Father Casey. He explained everything and the good priest was delighted that happiness was coming Ina's way. He knew how she had nursed her old father for many years before his demise.

From there Wullie hurried along to the Calton Social Club. Big Alex was busy sweeping the floor.

"Hello, Wullie, whit gives?" Alex asked.

Wullie told him what had happened and Alex, too, was delighted for Ina. Sure, he would arrange things with the Bachles and he told Wullie not to worry about the catering, that he would fix it.

"It's no' only Fingers McGeachie, y'know, who's got connections," Alex said, tapping his cheek with his forefinger.

Curdy McVey checked his diary to make sure he had no customers needing transport on the given day.

No, he assured Wullie, barring accidents he had a free day and his hearse was at Wullie's disposal. As the weeks passed everything fell into place.

Wullie asked Fingers McGeachie if he would his 'Best Man' and Fingers said he would be delighted as it was well past his time for acquiring a new suit. It was arranged, once more, that Annie would be Ina's 'Best Maid'

"Only wan thing oot o' place here," Wullie said to Ina as they sat going through the guest list.

"Whit's that?" Ina said, knitting her brows.

"Who's gonny gie ye away? Ah mean, AH canny walk doon the aisle and haund ye ower tae masel'."

Ina laughed. "Don't worry. Jist leave that tae me. Ah'll arrange that masel."

Wullie shrugged. "Okay," he said. "Jist as long as it's no' yer faither's ghost!"

Ina laughed. "Naw...naw," she said. "He's away back tae Paradise."

"Oh, he's a Celtic supporter, is he?" Wullie grinned.

"Naw, he prefers Shawfield," Ina said.

"Ah should've known dugs was his gemme, Wullie said and they both laughed.

The wedding day came around very quickly and the war was forgotten for a brief spell. Besides Ina, Annie was the happiest woman in the Calton.

Mrs Cominsky, from up 'The Paddy' close had presented Ina with a patchwork quilt.

"It's ze most beautul van I haff ever made," she said in her rich, Polish accent. "Ah got ze patches frae a jumble sale at Balmoral, as the Quuen haunded me the two hunner patches she said zat it vas a rich qvilt zat was a veddink present to her then her dugs got tae work on it. Zen it vas just patches. Noo it ezz a qvuilt again for you, Vee Ina and Vullie."

Ina was thrilled to think that she would be lying under a quilt that once covered the king and queen.

Wullie laughed, "Ah know you'll be shy on oor first night, Ina, " he said. "But don't worry. If yer face goes red Ah'll just call it a Royal Flush."

"Oh, Wullie," Ina cooed and dug an elbow into his side.

"C'mon youse two, " Annie snapped. "Time tae get ready. You, intae yer hoose, Ina, and YOU," she said to Wullie, "intae yer room."

The two went their separate ways. Wullie had already tried on his H.L.I. uniform and was delighted to find that it still fitted. Perhaps the McKenzie tartan kilt was just a little tight. But not enough to discard it.

Annie looked in the mirror and put the final touches to her make-up. Rita stepped into the room and stopped, "Aw, Mammy, ye look lovely!" she exclaimed.

Annie blushed.

"Aye, it's a nice wee suit Ah got at Madame Ashe's." Annie said, pleased with her outfit. "This'll be the last time Ah'll wear it until yer faither comes hame and the War's ower."

"Aw ye'll need tae wear it for the Christenin', mammy," Rita cried.

"Whit Christenin'?" Annie said quickly.

"Don't get yer hopes up, Mammy," Rita said. "But ye never know, dae ye?"

"Well that's another thing tae look forward tae," Annie laughed.

Rita, too, looked beautiful in a silk, lilac dress and hat.

Annie kissed her daughter. "Ye look like ye just stepped oot o' a catalogue, hen," Annie said proudly.

"Good looks run in tha faimily, Mammy," Rita said, giving her mother a playful dig in the ribs.

Wullie stepped out of his room, clicked his heels and smartly saluted.

"Aw, Uncle Wullie," Rita cried and threw her arms around his neck.

"No' bad, eh?" Wullie said. Wullie had always been proud of his uniform. He looked into the mirror, stepping back to get a fuller view. He saw himself in the smart uniform and then he saw Wee Sandy McSween and Big Peter McEwan and Tommy Wallace and Wullie brushed the corner of his eye.

He turned quickly as Ina walked into the room. She looked stunning in her powder-blue gabardine two-piece suit and the hat with the veil. Annie screamed.

"OOT...OOT, " Annie yelled. "It's bad luck for the 'groom tae see ye before ye get tae the altar!"

"Ach, Ah don't believe a' that rubbish," Ina said. "And, besides, Wullie seen me th...er...last time Ah wore this... remember?"

Annie surrendered. "Ah suppose so," she said.

Annie took Ina's hand, "How ur ye feelin', hen?" she asked.

"Ah'm very happy, Annie," Ina said.

"How dae ye feel...aboot Charlie, Ah mean?" Annie said.

"Ah DID like Charlie...but...!"

"Who's gien' ye away, Ina?" Rita asked.

"Ah've taken care o' that," Ina said.

"Who is it?" Rita repeated.

"You'll see," Ina said with a mischievous smile.

Annie tapped the side of her cheek with her finger and narrowed her eyebrows. "Noo," she said, "whit wis it that yer faither said aboot yer weddin' day durin' his Earthly appearance? Ye'd go doon the aisle cairryin' a horse shoe on thae airm of a man in a white uniform, that right?"

Ina nodded, "Ah think so," she said.

The door flew open and Fingers McGeachie stormed in. He went to the centre of the floor and did a quick pirouette, his arms outstretched.

"How dae Ah look, then, eh? Eat yer heart oot Errol Flynn!

And would ye look at youse three...Betty Grable, Lana Turner and Rita Hayworth!"

"Ye're a right charmer, Fingers," Annie said.

"Weddin's ur great, int they?" Fingers said.

"They're that great that ye never took the plunge yersel', Fingers?" Rita said.

"Oh but Ah did...wance."

"Whit happened?" Annie said.

"Ma wife ran away wi' a bookie's runner," Fingers said.

"Ye'd be broken hearted, Fingers?" Ina commiserated.

"Naw, naw," Fingers laughed. "She used tae drive me daft every night takin' her nail varnish aff. A' that screamin'!"

"Whit was she screamin' for?" Rita asked, puzzled.

"She used a blow lamp," Fingers said with a cheeky smile.

"Aw, ye're a case, Fingers!" somebody cried.

"Ye never fancied gettin' married again, then?" Annie said.

"Ah very nearly did, wance," Fingers said. "Ah'd got a haud

o' a lovely diamond engagement ring and there was this lassie Ah fancied."

"Whit happened?" Annie went on, her curiosity roused.

"Well," Fingers continued, "the night Ah was tae meet her and gie her the ring, Ah showed it tae this bloke in the pub and he made me an offer for it that Ah couldnae refuse. So Ah selt it tae him an' bought masel' a Crombie coat!"

"Whit a shame!" Ina said.

"No' really," Fingers said. "HE married her."

Everybody laughed and Fingers did another twirl.

"How dae like the gear?" he said.

Fingers was garbed in a top quality, obviously a Saville Row, dark blue suit.

"Yer suit's gorgeous!" everybody exclaimed. "Where did ye get it, Fingers?"

"Ah went roon' tae Paddy's," Fingers said.

"Paddy's Market?" Annie quizzed.

"Naw, Paddy Dolan's," Fingers said.

"THE LORD PROVOST'S?" Everyone cried out loudly.

"Ah left his chain," Fingers said cheekily. "Ah didnae want tae look ostentatious, know whit Ah mean? Take the glitz aff the bride."

"Ye're a' heart, Fingers, "Ina said and pecked his cheek. "And Ah owe ye a loat."

Fingers blushed, "If Ah can help somebody...." he began.

"A'right, we know the rest, Fingers," Annie said, cutting him off.

Fingers clapped his hands together. "Well, Ina, who's gien' ye away noo that yer escort has become yer 'groom?"

All turned at a loud knock on the door.

"That'll be him noo," Ina said as Annie answered.

Erchie McPherson walked in. He wore the full dress uniform of a City of Glasgow police constable, with the standard issue helmet. He pulled on his white gloves.

"Hello, Hello, Hello," he laughed. "Aw, ye look lovely, Ina," he said with a slight gasp. "Youse a' dae...even you, Fingers. That suit ye're wearin', funny but it matches the description o' wan that was nicked oot the Lord Provost's room in the City Chambers."

"Wis it in a big mahogany wardrobe wi' brass haun'les shaped like lyons heids?"

"Exactly!" Erchie said.

"Naw, know nothin' aboot it," Fingers said.

Erchie narrowed his eyes but said nothing. Turning to Wullie, he said, "Would ye look at YOU, Wullie! Ye look like ye just stepped oot o' Gunga Din!"

"Aye, well that's a smart uniform ye're wearin' yersel, Erchie. Ah see ye're wearin' the regulation polis's regulation helmet? Don't tell me ye've been accepted intae the regular force?"

Erchie pushed his thumbs through his tunic pockets and went up on his toes. "Aye, Ah have that!" he said proudly. "It's amazin' Ah was called intae the Chief Superintendent's oaffice and he telt me that the Chief Constable, Mr Sillitoe, had, on his recommendation, agreed for to waive the height restriction in ma case and allow me for to join the regulars." He glanced at Fingers, who whistled softly, looked at the ceiling and ran his fingers down under his lapels.

He would have no trouble from Erchie regarding his suit.

"Good for you, Erchie!" Annie said. "It was probably tae dae wi' you takin' in that German pilot ye caught!"

Erchie said nothing but glanced over at Fingers who winked. A chorus of 'Congratulations' followed. Wullie took Ina by the arm and led her to the corner of the room, saying to the assembled crowd, "Excuse me a minute folks!"

"Canny wait, eh, Wullie?" Fingers said cheekily.

Wullie didn't answer.

"Whit is it, Wullie?" Ina asked worriedly.

"Whit aboot Charlie, Ina?" Wullie said.

"Whit aboot Charlie, Wullie?"

"Well, Ah mean ye canny jist jump frae wan bidegroom tae another within a few weeks, jist like that," Wullie said.

"Wullie," Ina said, squeezing his hand, "Ah did like Charlie. Ah'm no' gettin' any younger an you wurnae interested. God knows Ah tried everythin' tae get you tae be interested in me. A' Ah ever got was sarcasm. When Charlie asked me tae mairry him Ah jist saw ma chance for a hame and a family life. Whit was Ah tae dae?"

Ina was right and Wullie knew it.

"When Ah was rotten tae you it was just a defence Ah was puttin' up, Ina. Ah felt Ah wisnae ready for marriage. Annie's made me too comfortable here. But when Ah saw Ah was gonny lose you Ah could've kicked masel'." He shook his head.

"It was always you, Wullie, ALWAYS. You've had ma heart for years. We'll be awfu' happy together, Wullie."

Ina kissed Wullie tenderly and there was applause from the centre of the room.

"Well," Annie said, "everythin' yer faither said is nearly true, Ina. Ye UR gonny walk doon the aisle. But no' wi' a man in a white uniform. He got it wrang there. Erchie's uniform could-nae be mair blacker!"

"Naw, naw," Erchie said, "Auld Jake was a stubborn auld cuss. He'd swear Black was white. So maybe he's right, right enough."

"Well he was nearly right," Annie said. "But nae horse shoe."

"Och, that disnae matter!" Ina said. "Ah'm no' superstitious!"

There was a sudden knock at the door.

"Come in!" Annie yelled, "it's open."

The door slowly opened and a head appeared round it. It was Charlie Gallagher. Annie's anger began to come to the surface and Ina noticed.

"Don't say anythin', Annie," she said quickly.

Charlie entered, his eyes firmly staring at the floor.

"Ah'll no' blame ye if ye want tae throw me doon the stairs, Ina," he said.

"Jist say whit ye've got tae say, Charlie," Ina said coldly.

"Ah didnae mean....Ah didnae mean..." Charlie did not finish the sentence.

"Here," he said. "Daisy shed a shoe comin' roon' the coarner. Ah...Ah thought ye might like it for good luck..."

Ina and Annie glanced at each other and smiled. Ina took the horse shoe from Charlie.

"Thank ye, Charlie," she said.

"And thank yer hoarse...for EVERYTHING," Wullie said.

Charlie nodded and, head bowed left the room.

Wullie signalled to Fingers to join him in the corner.

"That...er...that other wee favour, Fingers?"

"Nae bother, Wullie," Fingers said, producing a little parcel no bigger than a match box, from his pocket. "Here", he said.

Wullie gave him a playful punch on the shoulder.

"Ina," Wullie said, going towards his bride. "A wee weddin' present for you, hen."

Ina excitedly tore open the parcel. Her eyes widened.

"A pair of earrings...real diamonds!" she screamed in delight.

"Ah hivnae peyed for them yet," Wullie said in way of an apology.

"Efter the war, Wullie, efter the war," Fingers winked.

"Aw, Wullie!" Ina cried, "Ye remembered!" She threw her arms around him and pressed a kiss hard against his lips. The door was suddenly flung open and Rasputin hurried in.

"Raspy!!" Rita cried, throwing herself into his arms. "Bu... but how...how...?"

"Ah telt them ma best freen' was gettin' married and Monty arranged for me tae have compassionate leave. In fact he telt me he widnae say anythin' if Ah didnae come back."

Rita was delirious and kissed him all over.

"And guess who Ah met oan the stair oot there?" Rasputin cried and stepped aside.

Sammy, arm in a sling, his head swathed in bandages and propped up on one crutch hopped in.

"SAMMY!!!" Annie screamed, rushing forward and embracing him.

The blast of a horn made them hurry to the window. Curdy McVey waved up. He pointed to his gleaming hearse and all laughed.

Annie, Ina, and Erchie crammed into the cabin and Curdy drove off.

Fingers, Rita, Rasputin, Sammy and Wullie stood at the close and watched the hearse vanish round London Road.

"Whit dae we dae?" Rita said gloomily. "Walk?"

"Where is your faith, hen?" Fingers scoffed. "Dae you think Fingers McGeachie has retired?" With that he took a whistle from his pocket and gave two loud blasts.

Rita's mouth fell as a huge, pink American Cadillac dripping in chrome turned the corner. Rita threw her arms around Fingers' neck. Behind the wheel was a young G.I. in full dress uniform.

"It balangs tae a Yankee General, Ah know," Fingers said. "He's steyin' at the Beresford and he's awfu' partial tae a Single Malt. All laughed loudly as they piled in. This is Hank," he said, introducing the driver.

"Whit a shame!" Rasputin said. "Of a' the nice saints names tae choose frae— Benedict, Francis, Dominic...your maw called ye efter a dod o' wool."

"That's rich comin' frae you, Rasputin!" Fingers said.

Ina and Wullie stepped out of St Alphonsus' Chapel as man and wife. Curdy McVey opened wide the cabin door of the hearse saying, "At least it's clean, Ina!" But before they could step in, Fingers McGeachie stepped forward.

"Naw" he said. "This is your car!" He escorted them to the luxurious limousine, saw them comfortably settled and closed the door.

Everyone piled into the hearse and, singing loudly headed for the Calton Social Club.

Wullie and Ina were last to arrive and, stepping through the doors, they were met by all their guests who shouted greetings. Big Alex stepped forward with a tray containing two glasses of Malt Whisky and The Bachles struck up "Here Comes the Bride". Wullie and Ina each took a glass and Ina kissed Wullie softly on the cheek. She had landed her man! She was the happiest woman in the world. Except maybe for Annie who had her Sammy back with her.

Annie hid a tear and, glass in hand, stepped forward, kissed Wullie on the cheek and, looking into Ina's gloriously happy eyes, said.

"Congratulations, hen." Then, taking a step back, she raised her glass and, smiling happily, said, "Tae you, Ina, Happy Landings!"